THE DOCTOR
JOKE BOOK

THE DOCTOR
JOKE BOOK

Sid Berman

BARNES
&NOBLE
BOOKS
NEW YORK

This edition published by Barnes & Noble Books, Inc.,
by arrangement with James Charlton Associates.

1995 Barnes & Noble Books

Design and typography by Noble Desktop Publishers

Cover design by Kevin McGuinness

Cover cartoon by Leo Cullum

ISBN 1-56619-679-5

Printed and bound in the United States of America

M 9 8 7 6 5 4

For assisting me with jokes, cartoons, and stories, I want to thank a number of folks including Sam Gross, Leo Cullum, Henry Martin, Brian Savage, Tim Charlton, Roger Kepler, Lenore Binswanger, Blake Lochrie, Mike Mackerer, Henny Youngman, Jim Fitzgerald, Scott Carson, Bill Thompson, Lucianne Goldberg, and Frank Hoffman.

Be suspicious of any doctor who tries to take
your temperature with his finger.
                                    David Letterman

Mr. Rasmussen returned from an extended trip
and, not feeling well, visited his doctor. The
doctor performed a series of tests on him and
the patient was instructed to return in a few
days for the results.

When the man returned the doctor sat him
down. "Mr. Rasmussen, I have some bad news
for you. The tests show that you have bubonic
plague, Legionnaires' disease, TB, and leprosy."

Rasmussen was shocked and slumped down in
his chair. "Doctor, what do you recommend?"

The doctor said, "I think you should enter the
hospital immediately. We have an isolated
building here where a room has been prepared
for you. And we have a special diet for you of
flounder and pancakes."

"Flounder and pancakes?" gasped Mr. Rasmussen. "Will that help?" "No," replied the doctor, "but they're the only things I can think of to slide under the door."

Never go to a doctor whose office plants have died.

Erma Bombeck

The six-year-old was waiting at the hospital with his father, ..o was nervously pacing back and forth while his wife was in labor. The bored six-year-old struck up a conversation with another little boy.

"My dad tried to tell me that the stork doesn't bring babies. What a wild story *he* gave me!"

The longer I practice medicine, the more convinced I am there are only two types of cases: those that involve taking the trousers off, and those that don't.

Alan Bennett

A man accompanied by a German shepherd walked into the optometrist's office and sat down in the waiting room. A large officious receptionist looked up and growled, "Hey, there are no dogs allowed in here." She pointed to a sign on the wall, "Can't you read?"

"He's a Seeing Eye dog," the man replied.

"Oh well, that's different," she muttered.

A half-hour later, as the man was leaving the office, he passed a woman walking a Chihuahua on her way in to see the optometrist.

"They don't allow dogs in there," the man said.

"But you've got a dog," she protested.

"Yes, but I lied. I told the receptionist it was a Seeing Eye dog."

"Well, I'll try the same thing," she said sweetly.

The woman entered the office and was greeted with, "No dogs allowed in here. See the sign?"

"But I'm blind and this is my Seeing Eye dog."

"Are you trying to kid me?" snapped the receptionist. "That's a Chihuahua."

"Holy mackerel! You mean they gave me a *Chihuahua!?*"

"Who's the cute new doctor you're working with upstairs?" asked the nurse as she sat down to lunch with her friend.
"Dr. Harrison. He's a double-O seven doctor."
"Double-O seven?"
"Yes, licensed to kill."

My doctor is wonderful. Once, when I couldn't afford an operation, he touched up my X rays.
Joey Bishop

Intern to patient: "Did you know that diarrhea is hereditary?"
Patient: "Why no."
Intern: "Yes, it runs in your genes."

A man went to his doctor complaining that in the night he had swallowed his cat. The doctor was skeptical but decided to run some tests to placate the man. She probed and pinched, looked down the patient's throat, and finally took a series of X rays. Nothing indicated that there was a cat in the man's stomach. Still the patient insisted.
"Okay, then we'll just have to operate, and we can do it here in the office," said the doctor,

"A desire to 'be on the winning side,' Mr. Walsh, is not sufficient justification for a sex-change operation."

and gave the patient a shot. Seconds later he was dozing on the examination table. The doctor called her nurse and instructed him to go around the corner and borrow a cat from the market. When the man awoke the doctor held up the cat. "You were right!" she exclaimed.

The man looked up. "No, that's not it. My cat is gray!"

A young woman wasn't feeling well, and asked one of her co-workers to recommend a physician.

"I know a great one in the city, but she is very expensive. She charges $500 for the first visit, and $100 for each one after that."

Trying to save the cost of the initial fee, the woman breezed into the doctor's office and cheerily announced, "I'm back!"

Not fooled for a second, the doctor quickly examined her and said, "Very good. Just continue the treatment I prescribed on your last visit."

"Doctor, how do you have the nerve to charge me $200? All you did was paint my throat."

"What did you want for that? Wallpaper?"

Q. How do you hide a $100 bill from a neuro-surgeon?

A. Hide it in the charts.

Q. How do you hide a $100 bill from a plastic surgeon?

A. You can't.

A well-known Boston cardiologist was being interviewed by a reporter from a medical journal.

"Tell me, Doctor. You've had a long and distinguished medical career. Have you ever made a mistake?"

"Just one," the doctor sighed. "I once cured a millionaire in only three visits."

The doctor was making his hospital rounds and stopped by the bed of an attractive young woman. He looked her over then picked up her chart.

"What do you think, Doctor?"

"I think you have acute meningitis," he replied as he read her results.

"I'm sure I have. But what's *wrong* with me?"

"All right, now — the patient's lawyer will stand on the right side, and our lawyer will stand on the left side."

A man was standing in a long line at a movie theater when suddenly he felt someone massaging his shoulders.

He turned around to the woman behind him. "Hey lady, what do you think you're doing?"

"Oh, I'm sorry," she stammered. "You see, I'm a chiropractor and I could see that you were all tensed up, and so, without thinking, I started to rub your shoulders to release the tension and make you relax. I really apologize."

"Well, you ought to apologize," he blustered. "You shouldn't be taking your job out of the office. I'm a lawyer. Do you see me screwing the guy in front of me?"

An elderly doctor, well along in years, decided it was time to turn over his medical practice to his young son fresh out of internship. The son, though well-versed in the latest techniques at big city hospitals, was unfamiliar with the small town practice of his father so the old doctor decided to show him the ropes as he took his son around on his calls.

"One thing you always have to remember is that many times people won't tell you all you need to know to make a diagnosis," the old doctor lectured. "So we have to help them.

The first rule is that you must always be observant. For instance, Mrs. Johnson is overweight. But her problem isn't glandular: she stuffs herself with candy bars. I saw dozens of empty wrappers in her garbage when we were there this morning.

"Mr. Wade complains he has no energy. That's because he drinks his dinner. I had to climb over a mountain of scotch bottles to get into his house. So remember, be observant."

At the next stop the older doctor knocked. When there was no response, the two entered and went up the stairs to investigate. There they found a beautiful woman in bed with the sheets pulled up to her chin. The woman told them of her problem; she was having anxiety attacks. The young doctor bent over the patient and saw the beads of sweat on her forehead. He decided to check her temperature, but he clumsily fumbled the thermometer and it fell on the floor. He bent over and picked it up, and went on with his examination.

When he had finished, the examination he made his diagnosis. "I think you're getting too involved in politics. If you stop concentrating so much on that, I guarantee your attacks will subside." The woman sat up in her bed and nervously thanked him.

As the doctors got back to their car, the older one asked, "How on earth could you give her such specific advice?"

"Just followed your rule of simple observation and deduction," the young doctor answered confidently. "When I bent over to pick up the thermometer, I noticed the mayor under the bed."

One mouse to another: "I've got three brothers in psychological testing and a sister in heart research."

An elderly woman went to her pharmacist for some medicine.

"Now what was it?" she tried to recall. "All I can remember is that it was the same name as a bad woman."

The perplexed pharmacist looked around at her stock of over-the-counter drugs, but she was drawing a blank. Finally, she saw one that might fit the description and put it on the counter.

"Cortisone?"

God heals, and the doctor takes the fees.
Benjamin Franklin

"Doctor! Doctor! You have to see my wife right away! I think she has appendicitis!"

The doctor shook his head. "That's impossible! Your wife had her appendix out last year. Have you ever seen anybody with a second appendix?"

"Have you ever seen anybody with a second wife?"

Kevo the Great, a world famous magician, went to his doctor for an annual examination. After a series of routine tests and questions, the doctor asked the patient about his magic act. "What's your best trick?"

"Sawing a woman in half," replied Kevo.

The doctor was impressed. "That sounds really difficult."

"No, it's quite easy. I've been doing it since I was ten."

"Really. Are there any more at home like you?"

"Just a half sister."

The heart specialist looked in on his new patient, a Wall Street banker.

"We have some good news and bad news, Mr. Replogle," the doctor said.

"What is it?"

"The good news is that we've located a heart for the transplant. The bad news is that it belongs to a Democrat."

The very funny and quotable Abe Lemons, former college basketball coach, made a number of observations on the differences between a doctor and a coach. Here are a few:

— Doctors bury their mistakes. We still have ours on scholarship.

— Finish last in your league and they call you an idiot. Finish last in med school and they call you a doctor.

— Just once I'd like to see the win-loss records of doctors right out front where people can see them—won ten, lost three, tied two.

The dentist finished the routine oral examination of his patient, a wealthy Houston oilman. "Your teeth look perfect. We won't have to do anything this visit."

"I'm feeling lucky, Doctor. Go ahead and drill."

Did you hear about the two podiatrists who were arch rivals?

Dr. Rogers was striding down the hospital corridor when he crossed paths with Nurse Rollins.

"How was your vacation in Alaska, Doctor?" she asked sweetly.

"Terrible," he snarled. "I didn't kill a thing."

"You should've stayed here!"

It was the night before surgery and Mr. Greenfield had left his dinner untouched.

"At least eat your dessert," advised the nurse, pointing to the Jello on the tray.

Greenfield shook his head. "I don't want to eat anything more nervous than I am."

"The cracks can be fixed —
it's your cholesterol level that worries me."

Mrs. Rogovin was talking to one of her friends on the telephone. Her favorite subject for discussion was herself, with her son a close second. Mrs. Rogovin blathered on, "You'd never guess what what my son is doing. He's going to a psychiatrist three times a week. I'm so pleased."

Her friend on the other end said, "You're pleased that your son is going to a psychiatrist?"

"Sure," Mrs. Rogovin said, "and he's spending an incredible amount of money to do it."

Her friend was still just as confused and asked, "Why on earth does that make you happy?"

"Well," Mrs. Rogovin said grandly, "from what he tells me, he spends all that time just talking about me!"

A young doctor went to look at a practice that was for sale in a remote part of West Virginia. The situation seemed perfect: comfortable house, fully equipped lab, lovely gardens. The old doctor quoted a very affordable price.

"This looks great," said the young doctor. "But how could you get such a nice set up in an area where there's so few people?"

"It is just simple common sense and a strong work ethic," said the doctor. "For example, most people around here take a few weeks vacation. But my wife and I spend the time at home, gardening and putting things in order. The herb garden gives us a big harvest, and we mix the herbs and boil them into my secret tonic."

"But that doesn't really explain this fine house and all of this land," said the young man.

The doctor continued, "When the people come back from vacation, I tell them, 'You don't look too good. Is anything wrong?' And they usually say something like 'Well, vacation took a lot out of me.'

"'I know what you mean,' I tell them. 'Why don't you come by my office and I'll give you some of my good old fashioned tonic.' At $10 a bottle it really adds up.

"A few weeks after the patient buys the tonic, I tell them, 'You know, Mrs. So-and-so, you are looking much better.' That way they feel like the medicine is working. Then I have them in for a checkup, just to make sure everything is all right, and I tell them to bring a specimen. That way, you see, I get all my bottles back."

The two young boys were discussing their ailments together in the children's ward.

"Are you medical or surgical?" asked the first, who had been in the ward for a week.

"I don't know what you mean," replied the second.

"It's simple," replied the first. "Were you sick when you came in here? Or did they make you sick when you got here?"

A very sexy-looking blonde sauntered into the doctor's waiting room. The office was full of patients and she looked around in vain for an empty seat. Finally she walked over to one man and said in a low husky voice, "I wonder if I might trouble you for a seat. You see, I'm pregnant."

The man quickly stood up and offered his chair to the young woman. As she sat down he looked her over admiringly and commented, "I must say you certainly don't look pregnant. How far along are you?"

She looked up and smiled. "Oh, it's only been half an hour."

The desire to take medicine is perhaps the greatest feature which distinguishes man from animals.

William Osler

A man walked into the office of the eminent psychiatrist Dr. Von Bernuth, and sat down to explain his problem.

"Doctor, Doctor," he started.

"No need to repeat yourself, my good man," replied the doctor. "One 'doctor' is enough."

"Yes, well, you see, I've got this problem," the man continued. "I keep hallucinating that I'm a dog. A large white hairy Pyrenees mountain dog. It's crazy. I don't know what to do!"

"A common canine complex," said the doctor soothingly. "Come over here and lie down on the couch."

"Oh no, Doctor. I'm not allowed up on the furniture."

Q. Doctor, Doctor. My ankle hurts. What should I do?

A. Limp.

Dentist: drilling, filling, billing.
Steve Friedman

25

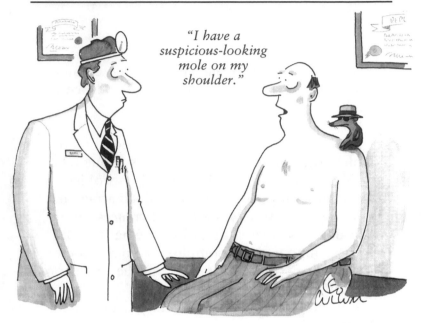

"I have a suspicious-looking mole on my shoulder."

The two fathers were peering at their new babies through the glass in the maternity ward. The younger of the two men proudly announced that the little baby girl was his first child, to which the other replied that the little baby boy was his fifth child.

"Fifth!" the first man exclaimed. "Wow! Well, since you've been here before let me ask you a very personal question. How long after the baby's born can my wife and I make love?"

The second man looked over. "That all depends on whether you have a private or semi-private room."

Patient to his psychiatrist: "I can't help it, Doctor. I keep thinking that my inferiority complex is bigger and better than anyone else's."

A poor carpenter took his ailing wife to a doctor. The doctor examined her, put her through a barrage of tests, and then pulled the man aside.

"Your wife is very sick and I'm afraid she might not have long to live. I can try and cure her but it will be very expensive," the doctor explained. "Do you have any insurance?"

The distraught man looked at him, "No. But if you cure her, I'll pay you anything. Anything!"

"But I could treat her and she still might die," said the doctor shrewdly.

"Just treat her," the man pleaded. "Whether you cure her or kill her, I'll pay you whatever you ask even if I have to sell everything."

The doctor agreed, but despite his treatment, the woman passed away within the week. Remembering the conversation, the doctor presented a huge bill to the grieving carpenter.

"Ten thousand!" the carpenter gasped. "I can't possibly pay this. Can't we go to the judge in town and discuss some form of settlement?"

The doctor agreed. That afternoon the doctor, carpenter, and judge sat down to discuss the fee. First the judge heard from the carpenter. Then he turned to doctor. Well aware of the doctor's reputation for large fees, the judge asked, "Did you cure this man's wife?"

"Alas, no," replied the doctor, sadly shaking his head.

"Did you kill her?"

"Certainly not," protested the doctor.

"Well, under what terms of the agreement are you claiming a fee?"

I learned a long time ago that minor surgery is when they do the operation on someone else, not you.

Bill Walton

The psychiatrist was examining a patient. "Now tell me again, Mr. Oberbeck, what do you do for a living?"

"I build homes. I built a million last year."

The therapist shook his head. "You know that's a lie."

"Fabricated."

A sickly man dragged himself into the doctor's waiting room to get the results of tests that had been performed on him a week earlier. He slumped painfully into a chair and then looked around at the only other patient waiting, a woman. And what a woman! A gorgeous brunette, in a short slinky dress which did nothing but accentuate her magnificent figure.

He had never seen such a spectacular-looking woman and he couldn't keep his eyes of her. Her looks almost took his mind off his fears about the test results. Soon the doctor came out.

"Mr. Johnson, the test results have come back and I've got some good news and some bad news."

"What's the bad news?" the man gasped.

"The bad news is that all the tests show that you're going to die within a month."

"Oh, that's terrible," the man wailed, "then what's the good news?"

"See that great-looking woman? I'm having an affair with her."

The young woman looked up from her hospital bed at the handsome doctor who was examining her patient's report. She fluttered her eyelids and said breathlessly, "They tell me, Doctor, that you're a real lady killer."

The doctor smiled and shook his head. "No, I can assure you. I make no distinction between the sexes."

On his first visit to the psychiatrist, Mr. Bakalar was given the Rorschach ink blot analysis. The doctor showed him the first picture and asked him what it looked like.

"That's two dogs having sex," replied Mr. Bakalar.

Of the second ink blot, the man commented, "That is a nude woman in the shower."

On the third one, the man said, "That is a pair of crotchless underpants."

The entire test continued in this manner, and when it was complete, the doctor put the cards in a pile and looked at the patient, "Mr. Bakalar, you do seem very preoccupied with sex."

"Me?!" Mr. Bakalar answered. "You're the pervert who keeps showing me all the dirty pictures!"

"My stomach has been bothering me, Doctor," complained the patient.

"What have you been eating?" asked the doctor.

"That's easy. I only eat pool balls."

"Pool balls?!" said the astonished doctor. "Maybe that's the trouble. What kind do you eat?"

"All kinds," replied the man, "Red ones for breakfast, yellow and orange ones for lunch, blue for afternoon snacks, and purple and black for dinner."

"I see the problem," said the doctor. "You haven't been getting any greens!"

A concerned woman called the family doctor and explained that her husband was very ill.

"I know this is a lot to ask, Doctor," pleaded the woman, "but we live far from town and the car is broken and my husband is quite sick. Is it possible for you to come out here?"

"No problem," boomed the doctor. "I have another patient to visit in the neighborhood. I'll just kill two birds with one stone!"

A man with a terrible stuttering problem finally went to his doctor, who recommended a specialist. The specialist worked with the man for six weeks. Finally, the man could say, "Peter Piper picked a peck of pickled peppers" without a stutter. The specialist presented him with a bill and told him to report back in two weeks.

"How did your two weeks go?" asked the doctor upon the patient's return.

"Nnot tttto well," said the man. "Yyou dddon't know how hhhard it is to wwwork into a ccconversation 'Peter Piper picked a peck of pickled peppers.'"

A man went to the hospital complaining of sharp pains in his legs. After a few days of tests, his doctor came to see him. "Mr. Strong, I have some good news and some bad news for you. Which do you want first?"

Strong asked for the bad news first.

"The bad news is that we'll have to amputate both your legs."

"My legs!" cried the man. "What on earth could the good news possibly be?"

"The man across the hall says he'll buy your slippers."

Every invalid is a physician.
Irish proverb

A doctor and a lawyer were talking at a party.

"You know, Barry," said the doctor, "I hate it when people come up to me at a party and tell me what's wrong with them. Then they expect me to dish out free advice right on the spot. Does that ever happen to you?"

"All the time," assured the lawyer.

"What do you do?"

"Well, the next morning I send them a bill that reads 'Fees incurred at party last night—$25.' That soon stops it."

"That's a good idea. I'll try it!"

The next morning the doctor received a letter from the lawyer which read, "Fees incurred at party last night—$25."

At a cocktail party, Gutowsky, the well-known internist, was asked the secret of her success.

"It's easy," she replied. "When a patient comes in with stomach problems, I ask them if they play golf. If they say yes, I tell them to stop. If they say no, I tell them to start."

"I'd like to help you, but you're in a different H.M.O."

Mr. Norton was in the hospital recovering from an operation when the nurse on duty received a call from a man who asked how Mr. Norton was doing.

"Oh, quite well. We expect he'll be released in the morning."

"Very good, thank you."

"May I asked who is calling so that I can tell Mr. Norton?" inquired the nurse.

"This *is* Mr. Norton. The doctors don't tell me a damn thing!"

Mr. Kelly walked into his doctor's office to hear the results of some tests that he had undergone the previous week. He asked anxiously, "Dr. Mirsky, give it to me straight. What do the tests say?"

Shaking his head, the doctor replied, "Well, to be honest with you, Mr. Kelly, you only have six months to live."

"Oh my God!" said Kelly, slumping down in his chair. "Is there anything I can do?"

The doctor thought for a moment. "Only one thing I can think of. Marry an ugly woman with three hyperactive children, and move to Detroit."

The patient was confused. "Will that help me live longer?"

"No," replied the doctor, "but it will sure seem like it."

Eric was in the midst of a very competitive table tennis match when he accidentally caught a slammed ball in the mouth and swallowed it. Gasping for air, he was rushed to the emergency ward of the local hospital where surgery was performed.

When Eric awoke several hours later he looked down up at the doctor and thanked him for saving his life. Then he looked down and saw about twelve sewn up incisions on his stomach.

"Good gosh!" exclaimed the patient. "Why did you make so many cuts?"

The doctor spread his palms. "That's the way the ball bounces."

A man in his seventies was walking down the street when he encountered an old friend of his who was accompanied by his wife.

"Hey, you two. Good to see you," he hailed, and shook hands. "Harry, you look terrific. Tell me, anything come of that diagnosis that you might have Alzheimer's?"

"Ben, I've been going to this new doctor and he's given me some experimental medication to go along with some physical therapy. And it's worked wonders. I'm completely cured!"

"Harry, that's great news. What's this doctor's name?"

Harry frowned for a moment. "Ben, what's that flower called? You know, it's usually red, and has a long stem, and thorns?"

"You mean a rose?"

Harry nodded and turned to his wife. "Rose, what's that doctor's name?"

Ted Giannoulas, the man who portrayed the San Diego Chicken, was asked if his mother thought his choice of profession foolish: "Not at all. She thinks I'm a doctor in Wisconsin."

Dr. Lochrie was attending a dinner party and watching the host adroitly carve and slice the large turkey for his guests.

"How am I doing, Doctor? Pretty good, huh! I think I'd make a pretty good surgeon," said the host proudly.

When the host was through piling up the sliced turkey on the serving platter, the good physician observed, "Anyone can take them apart. Now let's see you put it back together again."

The doctor was trying to comfort a sick patient, who seemed distraught about his ailment.

"You know, Henry, you shouldn't be nervous. I've had the same thing myself."

"Yes, but you didn't have the same doctor!"

Roscoe and his pregnant wife, Ellen, were ranchers in Wyoming and lived miles and miles from the nearest town. One evening, while he and his wife were finishing up in the barn, the labor pains began. Collapsing on a bale of hay, Ellen cried out, "I can't move. Call the doctor in Sheridan. The baby's coming!"

Roscoe raced to the house and dialed the doctor, who assured him he would be there in twenty minutes. He told Roscoe to keep his wife warm and not try to move her. Roscoe rushed back to the barn and, minutes later, the doctor arrived. Directing the distraught husband to hold a light over the prostrate woman, the doctor swiftly performed his ministrations.

"Hold the light a little closer now, Roscoe," the doctor ordered. "There! I'd like to congratulate you. You're the father of a beautiful baby boy!"

"Thank you so much doctor," Roscoe gasped emotionally.

"Wait a minute, hold the light a little closer again," instructed the doctor. "Well, well! Now you're the father of two brand new baby boys." The doctor proudly held up the latest arrival.

"Thank you so much, Doctor," said Roscoe, backing away to a corner of the barn.

"Not so fast, Roscoe, bring the light a little closer. Make that three boys!" the doctor said triumphantly, as he pulled another little head through.

"Well, Doc, thanks, I guess." Roscoe began to turn the light out.

"Wait a minute, Roscoe, bring the lamp back over," the doctor motioning said.

"Excuse me, Doctor," Roscoe demurred, "but don't you think it might be the light that keeps attracting them?"

A doctor called his patient and said, "I have some bad news and some very bad news."

"Well, why don't we start with the bad news," answered the wary patient.

"You only have twenty-four hours to live," replied the doctor.

"What," gasped the patient. "That's the *good* news! What could possibly be worse than that?"

"I've been trying to reach you since yesterday!"

A man was sitting up in his hospital bed while his wife was opening his get well cards.

"This card says 'Get Well Quick.' It's from our hospitalization plan!"

Two elderly women were having lunch together and the conversation was mainly on each of their ailments.

"It takes me nearly an hour to swallow all the pills the doctors have prescribed. And I have to do it three times a day."

"That's nothing," said the second. "I take a pill that has nothing but side effects!"

Q. What's the difference between God and a neurosurgeon?

A. God doesn't think he's a doctor.

The traveling salesman went to the doctor complaining of fatigue. After a routine series of tests, the doctor was a bit perplexed. "Well, the tests don't reveal anything, so let's take this from a new perspective. How often do you have sex?"

"Three times a night on Monday, Wednesday, Friday, and Saturday," replied the salesman.

"Oh, that explains it," said the doctor, "I suggest you take a rest on Wednesday."

"Oh, I couldn't do that, Doctor. That's the only night of the week that I'm home."

A famous heart surgeon died and went to heaven. When he arrived at the Pearly Gates he found himself at the end of a mile-long line. Not used to waiting for anything, the impatient doctor marched up to the gate and confronted St. Peter.

"Listen. Do you know who I am? I am Dr. Harris, the famous heart surgeon! I have saved hundreds of lives and I shouldn't be kept waiting!"

"Sorry, friend," answered St. Peter, "we get famous people here every day. Please go to the end of the line like everybody else."

Dr. Harris reluctantly retreated to the end of the queue. While shuffling his feet and growing increasingly impatient, he noticed a young intern go past the line and straight through the Pearly Gates. A furious Dr. Harris made his way back up to the head of the line and yelled at St. Peter. "How could you possibly let that scrawny young intern into heaven before a man of my stature?"

"That was no intern," corrected St. Peter. "That was God. He just likes to play doctor."

Two woman were at the theater watching a movie about a famous surgeon. One woman leaned over and whispered to her friend: "At the prices they charge, it's no wonder they wear masks."

Voice heard from the surgical team at the start of the operation: "Who opens?"

Some tortures are physical and some are mental, but the one that is both is dental.
Ogden Nash

"Doctor! Doctor!" cried out the man as he rushed into the doctor's office. "I think I have amnesia!"

The doctor was concerned. "When did you first notice it?"

"Notice what?"

A man walked into the doctor's office to find out the results of a series of tests that he had undergone. His worst fears were confirmed.

"I'm afraid I have some bad news for you, Mr. McIntosh. You're going to die in four weeks."

The man was distraught. "Doctor, that's terrible! I want a second opinion."

"Okay. You're ugly too."

A millionaire, well along in years, had a sharp pain in his chest. He turned to his wife and gasped, "I'm having a heart attack. Quick, buy me a hospital!"

The doctor finished his examination and told the patient to get dressed and to come into his office.

"Sit down, Mr. Kaysen. After looking at these test results, I recommend that you have an operation immediately."

The man thought for a moment. "How will this affect my hobby, Doctor?"

"What's your hobby?"

"Saving money!"

Two interns, Johnson and Fredricks, roomed together. They got along in ever respect except that Fredricks had a horrible smoking problem. Johnson lectured him again and again, "You know that smoking is unhealthy. If you don't take care of yourself, one night you're going to cough your guts out."

The next month Fredricks was to be married, and the roommates went out for one last night of bachelor fun. The two staggered back home, the groom-to-be much the worse of the two. Fredricks collapsed onto his bed and fell into a deep sleep. Johnson, as a joke, went to the lab at the hospital and grabbed up a sample of human intestines. He brought it home and dropped the intestines over his sleeping roommate's chest.

The next morning, Johnson was up early drinking coffee when the hungover roommate appeared in the doorway. "Did you sleep well?" Johnson inquired.

Fredricks looked pale. "The strangest thing happened. I think I actually did cough up my guts."

Johnson suppressed a smile. "Didn't I tell you to stop smoking? You could have avoided all this trouble."

His friend had a sick expression. "You don't know the half of it. After I noticed my intestines all over my chest, I had a heck of a time getting them back in."

Due to overcrowding in the restaurant, an elderly gentleman was forced to share his table with a quiet man in a dark suit. The senior citizen ordered a large sirloin, and when the waiter returned with it, the elderly man dug around in his bag looking for something.

"Oh no," he said disgustedly. "I seem to have forgotten my dentures and this delicious steak is going to go to waste."

Without a word, the other man rummaged through a leather valise next to him and pulled out a set of dentures. The older man, eager to eat the delicious steak, gratefully took the dentures and fit them in his mouth. But, alas, they were too small.

"Thanks, mister, it was a good try," he said regretfully, "I've got a hard mouth to fit for dentures."

His table companion nodded at the elderly gentleman, and without a word searched through his bag again. This time he produced a

"Let's work on the list of doctors who think they are God."

pair that fit perfectly. The grateful octogenarian thanked him and proceeded with his meal.

When he had finished the steak, the old man leaned back and sighed contentedly, "Thanks a lot. You know, you're the first person I've met who has given me an exact match for dentures. Where is your dentist's office and when can I get an appointment?"

"Oh no, I'm afraid you can't get an appointment," the man chuckled. "I'm not a dentist. I'm a mortician."

Mr. Jackson was having some troubling pains in his chest and went to his family doctor. After an initial series of examinations, the family physician was still perplexed, and recommended a specialist at the hospital. The specialist was consulted and performed further tests on Mr. Jackson. Finally, the doctor sat his patient down.

"I'm sorry to tell you this, Mr. Jackson, but you seem to have contracted an incurable disease. I'd give you inside of three months to live."

Jackson shook his head in disbelief. "Doctor, that's just not fair. I'm still a young man. I have a family, a wife, and two young children to support. Mortgage payments, school. Heck, I can't even come up with enough money to pay you in three months."

The doctor thought for a moment. "Okay, then I'll give you six months to live."

A woman went to see her psychiatrist. "Doctor, you've got to help me. I find that I'm talking to myself all the time. Everywhere. In elevators, on the street, at parties. What can I do?"

The doctor leaned back. "Oh, I wouldn't worry about it. Lots of people talk to themselves all the time. It's perfectly normal."

The woman shook her head. "Yes, but you don't know what a bore I am!"

A hospital bed is a parked taxi with the meter running.
> *Groucho Marx*
> *(also attrib. to Frank Scully)*

The patient was in the hospital recuperating after a quadruple bypass operation on his heart. The doctor had been visiting him every day for a week to see how the recovery was progressing. On this visit the patient was sitting up with his eyes open. Although still attached to numerous tubes and monitoring wires, the patient looked much improved.

"How are we feeling today?" Dr. Goldberg asked.

"I'm feeling much better, thank you, Doctor, and I'm ready for you to give me your bill."

"Not yet," cautioned the doctor. "I don't think you're strong enough."

Randy Potemkin, a world-renowned urologist and expert on sexual dysfunction, was asked by a women's group in his suburban town to give a lecture on his specialty. Giving his standard talk about sex was an easy request to fulfill, but he decided to give the lecture on sailing.

He knew very little about sailing, but had promised himself to take time out of his schedule to take up the sport. He went to the library and read about sailing, he borrowed videotapes on races, and he went by a local ship yard to observe firsthand some of the newer boats. But when he arrived at the auditorium to give the speech, Potemkin felt a moment of panic about lecturing on a subject he still knew little about. Instead, he gave his normal talk about sexual intercourse. The women were thrilled and applauded him wildly.

That afternoon, one of the women in the audience ran into Mrs. Potemkin at the market and gushed on about what a wonderful speech the doctor had given. "You must be very proud! Your husband is such a good speaker and is so knowledgeable about his subject."

Mrs. Potemkin was taken aback. "Knowledgeable? He's only done it twice. Once he got sick and the other time his hat blew off!"

Frank Hoffman, a retired baseball player, in poor health and down on his luck, was in need of an operation. He asked around and was finally directed to the most respected and expensive specialist in town.

"Doctor, I've been told that I need this expensive operation," Hoffman explained.

"I'm afraid it'll cost you $20,000. In advance," replied the doctor.

"What! But, Doctor, c'mon, times are tough, I didn't make the big bucks when I played so I can't afford that much," replied the old ball player.

"I'll tell you what I'll do," the doctor responded. "I used to be a big fan of yours. I'll call it a thousand and you send me one of your old uniforms."

"That's still too steep," replied Hoffman.

They haggled back and forth, and finally settled on $50 and the baseball cap the old timer wore in the World Series.

"At that price, I might as well do it for free!" said the doctor, shaking his head. "Tell me, if you knew I was the most expensive doctor in town, and you knew you couldn't afford it, why did you come here?"

"Hey, Doctor," replied Hoffman, "where my health is concerned, money is no object."

After six months of therapy with a patient, the psychiatrist could stand it no longer. "The smoking!" blurted out the therapist. "You've got to give up smoking!"

"Smoking?" replied the man. "Smoking is the key to my disorder?"

"No, of course not," said the doctor, "but at least you'll stop burning holes in my couch!"

Our doctor would never really operate unless it was necessary. He was just that way. If he didn't need the money, he wouldn't lay a hand on you.

Herb Shriner

A distinguished looking older man walked into a psychiatrist's office. When the psychiatrist began talking to him and filling out the preliminary forms, the man took out a pouch of tobacco, and began stuffing its contents into his ears.

The doctor looked up at him and said, "Well, sir, I think you have come to the right place for treatment. Is there anything I can do for you first?"

"Yes there is," said the man. "Do you have a light?"

A psychiatrist's ad in the paper read: "Positive results within a year or your mania back."

A blue-haired older woman waddled into the doctor's office and said, "Doctor, I don't feel so good."

The woman had been a patient of the doctor's for many years and he was very familiar with her list of ailments. "Mrs. Kralinski, some things even modern medicine can't cure. I can't make you any younger, you know."

"Who asked you to make me younger?" she answered. "All I want is for you to make me older!"

The old lion, King of the Jungle, went to see the jungle doctor about his problem with insomnia. A flock of birds had settled in his mane and were arguing so late into the night that he couldn't sleep. The jungle doctor told the lion to go home and put a pound of yeast in his pajamas and the birds would go away.

The old lion didn't believe it, but he did as he was told. Much to his surprise, the cure worked and the birds left the next night. He went to thank the jungle doctor, and offer some payment for the successful treatment.

"Oh, you don't need to worry about that!" answered the doctor, waving away the payment. "You are the King of the Jungle!"

"But surely you must need something to support yourself after your years of schooling?" growled the lion.

"No, this is all common sense," said the doctor. "Surely you know that yeast is yeast and nest is nest, and never the mane shall tweet!"

A very sexy young woman clad in a short skirt and revealing blouse reported to the city hospital for her scheduled operation. After the operation, the doctor was at her bedside and asked how she is feeling. "Very well, thank you, Dr. Karraker, but I was wondering if the scar will show?"

"My dear," replied the doctor, "that is entirely up to you."

A woman brushed past the nurse and grabbed the doctor's sleeve.

"Doctor! Doctor!" she cried. "My husband is a sex maniac! He wants to do it all the time. Before breakfast, after breakfast, on the way to work, during lunch, before dinner, after dinner, and then over and over again all night long.

Why, the other day he came up to me at the freezer and we were doing it again!"

The doctor looked at her. "The freezer doesn't sound any stranger than the other places you mentioned."

"At the supermarket?"

An exhausted-looking man dragged himself in to the doctor's office.

"Doctor, there are dogs all over my neighborhood. They bark all day and all night, and I can't get a wink of sleep!"

"I have good news for you," the doctor answered, rummaging through a drawer full of sample medications. "Here are some new sleeping pills that work like a dream. A few of these and your trouble will be over."

"Anything, doctor. I'll give it a shot."

A few weeks later the man returned, looking worse than ever.

"Doc, your plan is no good. I'm more tired than before!"

"I don't understand how that could be, said the doctor, shaking his head. "Those are the strongest pills on the market!"

"That may be true," the man answered wearily, "but I'm up all night chasing those dogs, and when I finally catch one it's hell getting him to swallow the pill!"

A psychiatrist to his patient: "You're right, there *is* a man following you. He's trying to collect my bill."

Mrs. Bernard, eight months pregnant, carefully made her way into the obstetrician's office and sat down.

"Doctor, you've got to help me. Every morning when I wake up I am sick and nauseous. The feeling doesn't go away for at least sixty minutes. What should I do?"

"Get up an hour later."

A young man got married to a famous and beautiful supermodel. In a rush to impress his new bride, the groom had made many improvements in their weekend house. In his haste, however, he forgot to tell his wife that he had lacquered the toilet seat, and when she used the bathroom she became glued to the seat. The distraught groom was forced to unbolt the toilet seat, wrap his bride in a raincoat and race to the emergency room of the local hospital. Speeding past a full waiting room, the man rushed her into the office of the doctor on duty, where the young bride reluctantly bared all.

"Well, what do you think?" asked the anxious groom.

"Very nice," clucked the doctor. "Really quite impressive. But why did you have it framed?"

The two women met for lunch, having both come directly from their psychiatrists' offices.

"I don't know what's the matter with me today," said the first. "I'm feeling a little bit schizophrenic."

"Well," said her friend, "that makes four of us!"

The maternity ward waiting room was full of anxious fathers-to-be pacing up and down. One nervous man blurted out to another standing across from him, "I am so annoyed! This had to happen on our vacation."

"Vacation?" said the other. "What about me? We were on our honeymoon!"

After a series of expensive tests and examinations on Mr. Dunne, the doctor threw up his hands and explained, "I can do nothing for you. Your problem is hereditary."

"Then send the bill to my father," snapped the patient.

"The ringing in your ears — I think I can help."

Drawing by Cullum;
© 1992 The New Yorker Magazine, Inc.

The doctor, making her rounds, walked into the semi-private room to examine old Mrs. Waxman. After the exam in her best professional voice, she said smoothly, "You are coughing much more easily this morning."

"I should," groaned the patient, "I've been practicing all night."

The doctor told me to get rid of my cold I should drink lemon juice after a hot bath. But I could never finish drinking the hot bath.

Bob Uecker

The husband and wife were in the waiting room when the doctor came out to see them.

"And what seems to be the problem with your husband, Mrs. Taylor?" asked the doctor.

The woman answered, "His problem seems to be that he's constantly worried about money."

"Ah," said the doctor, "I think we can relieve him of that."

The infirmary doctor was examining the college student and asked him to breathe in and out while he listened with a stethoscope.

"I see you've had some problems with angina pectoris," observed the doctor.

"You're right, Doctor," answered the young man, "but that wasn't her name."

The dentist leaned over the patient in the chair.

"Open... wider... wider... wider..."

Suddenly the patient sat up."Listen, if you're going to get in, I'm getting out!"

Mrs. Winston called as soon as she received the doctor's bill.

"I think you've overcharged me on this bill. My son Jimmy only had the flu."

"That's true," agreed the nurse. "But you brought him in here nearly a dozen times."

"I know. But you forget he infected the whole school."

After three days in a coma the man finally regained consciousness. He opened his eyes to find the doctor taking his pulse.

"You were at death's door, Mr. Winters," said the doctor gravely. "It's only your strong constitution that has pulled you through."

"I just hope you remember that, Doctor, when you send me your bill."

Difference between a neurotic and a psychotic:

A psychotic thinks that two plus two is five; a neurotic knows that two plus two is four—but he hates it.

The young man had been in the hospital for nearly a month and in that time had grown very fond of the pretty nurse in attendance. She had even responded a bit and, as part of his therapy, had kissed him several times. The young man was almost well enough to go home and this particular morning he grabbed the nurse's hand as she stood next to his bed.

"I'm desperately in love with you," he gasped. "I don't want to get well."

"Don't worry, you won't," said the nurse sweetly. "Your doctor's in love with me and he saw us kissing yesterday."

The patient sat in the chair as the dentist was busy adjusting his tools.
"I'll be with you in a minute," the dentist said. "I must run my drill first."
The patient looked up in astonishment. "Can't you fill a tooth without a rehearsal?"

The elderly patient looked up at the doctor and asked, "Doctor, how long am I going to live?"
"Don't worry," the doctor replied, "you should live to be eighty."
"But I am eighty," he answered.
"See, what'd I tell you."

A fashionable surgeon, like a pelican, can be recognized by the size of his bill.
                    J. Chalmers Da Costa

"Barbara, you look in great shape for a woman in her mid-sixties," the doctor pronounced. "And you know the best thing about turning sixty-five?"

"No, what?" asked Barbara.

"No more calls from insurance agents!"

A specialist is a doctor with a smaller practice and a bigger boat.

Tom Charlton

The bishop was sitting in the waiting room when a red-faced and crying nun ran by him from the doctor's inner office. The angry cleric charged into the office and demanded to know what the doctor had said.

"I told her she was pregnant," answered the doctor.

"It is certainly not true. Why would you possibly tell her something like that?" demanded the outraged bishop.

"So what," replied the doctor, "It sure cured her hiccups!"

During Mr. Smith's annual physical, the doctor asked him to lean out the window and then stick out his tongue.

"You ask me to do that every year, and I never know why."

"Oh, there's no medical reason," assured the doctor. "I just don't like my neighbors."

The dentist was examining the teeth of his new patient.

"Wow, you have got the biggest cavity I have ever seen! *The biggest cavity I have ever seen.*"

"There's certainly no need to repeat it," admonished the patient.

"I didn't," said the dentist. "That's the echo!"

An 91-year-old husband and his 85-year-old wife went to the doctor for physical exams.

"This is amazing," said the doctor, "Truly amazing. You are both in perfect health!"

"Good," replied the man. "Now we can get a divorce."

"A divorce!" exclaimed the doctor, "After all these years, how could you get a divorce now?"

"We wanted to wait until the children were dead."

"Doctor! Doctor! Will I be able to read after I get these glasses?"

"Oh, certainly," replied the doctor.

"Great! I could never read before."

At a cocktail party, the lawyer was getting annoyed at the number of people who kept asking for free advice. He asked his doctor friend if he had the same problem.

"All the time," agreed the doctor.

"Well, don't you get tired of it? What do you do?" asked the lawyer.

"There's a very simple solution, and I think it will work for you as well," said the doctor. "When they ask for advice, just tell them to undress!"

I've had the stitches color coded so the autopsy will be easier for everybody.

Football player Dan Hampton,
after his tenth knee operation

An expectant mother asked her doctor, "Will my husband be allowed to stay in the delivery room during the birth?"

"Oh yes, of course. I think it is very important that the father be present."

The woman gasped. "Oh no! I don't think we should let the father in. He and my husband don't get along too well!"

A famous surgeon was giving the commencement address to a graduating class of medical students. At the end of the speech, he conducted a question-and-answer session and one of the students asked him how he became so successful at medicine.

"When I started medical school, all I could think of was dancing," the eminent doctor began. "I would constantly call women to ask them out to dance. Except that every time I did, I wouldn't hear the end of it from my father. Eventually, every time I went towards the phone, he passed me a textbook. In the end, I forgot dancing and concentrated on my studies. I spent enough time at it that I graduated first in my class and became the success that I am today."

"Wow," said one student to the other, "The story of one of the world's great doctors."

"No," corrected a classmate. "The story of one of the world's worst dancers."

Mike said to his psychiatrist, "I can't get over this feeling that I was supposed to be born as a dog."

"How long has this been going on?" asked the psychiatrist.

"Since I was a puppy!"

The middle-aged married couple entered the doctor's office and both took seats.

"Doctor," said the woman to her psychiatrist, "everyone treats my husband like a parking meter!"

"Well, isn't he his own person? Why doesn't he speak up for himself?"

"He would, but his mouth is full of quarters!"

"Doctor! Doctor!" said the woman to her psychiatrist, "My husband thinks he is a refrigerator!"

"Why exactly does that bother you?"

"When he sleeps with his mouth open, the light keeps me up!"

Ms. Jones was interviewing a man about to be released from a mental hospital after ten years of therapy. "What do you think you'll do when you get out?" asked Ms. Jones.

"I think I may resume my law practice," said the patient, "or possibly finish my accounting degree. Then again, since I have a medical degree, I could pursue that. I could practice psychiatry and use all of the techniques that I have learned while I have been here."

Ms. Jones was impressed. "It sounds like you have a number of interesting choices."

"That's true. And if all else fails, I could be a tea kettle!"

The new secretary in the surgeon's office was enthusiastic, though inexperienced. She was busy keyboarding the doctor's notations he had written following an emergency operation. The secretary was puzzled by the notation: "Patient shot in the lumbar region." After a moment's hesitation, a smile creased her face and she typed, "shot in the woods."

The doctor answered the phone and heard the familiar voice of a colleague on the other end of the line. "We need a fourth for poker," said the friend.

"I'll be right over," whispered the doctor.

As he was putting on his coat, his wife asked, "Is it serious?"

"Oh yes, quite serious," said the doctor gravely. "Why, there are three doctors there already!"

A renowned doctor was addressing a class of graduating medical students. "Soon you will go out into the world," he said, "and you will have to weigh the cost of your education against the size of your fees. For myself, I felt it was best to specialize. Now I get $500 an hour for house calls, $200 an hour for office visits, and $100 for advice over the phone."

"Hey, Doctor," called out one of the students, "how much do you get if you pass one of your patients on the street?"

An aging and still haughty doctor called one of his assistants into the office. "You know, I've had a marvelous and unique life," he said expansively. "But I'm getting along in years and I think it is time I thought about my demise. I'd like you to go out and find a nice resting place for me."

A few days later the assistant returned with pictures of a cemetery site on the side of a hill, one with a southern exposure and a stream nearby.

"This looks wonderful!" beamed the doctor. "How much is it?"

"Well, sir, this lot is $400,000."

"It's $400,000! But I'm only going to be there three days!"

A doctor's life is a tough one. He may be called off the golf course at a moment's notice.
Jeff Lydon

There are only two sorts of doctors: those who practice with their brains, and those who practice with their tongues.

Sir William Osler

A gray-haired woman went to the doctor complaining of swollen ankles. The doctor gave her anti-swelling pills and instructed her to take one every other day.

"I'm sorry, Doctor," said the lady. "I'm not sure I understand the treatment."

"It is very simple," said the doctor. "Take one pill today, skip tomorrow, take one pill the next day, skip the day after that, and continue that way until the prescription is finished. Come back and see me then."

A few weeks later the woman returned, and her ankles looked completely normal. The doctor was pleased. "It looks like it worked. I think you can stop the treatment."

"Oh, good," said the old woman. "I didn't mind the pills, but the skipping was killing me!"

The doctor was trying to determine exactly what was the matter with the patient.

"Do you feel listless, Mr. Corbin?"

"No, I don't feel listless, Doctor. If I felt that good, I wouldn't be here."

Two psychiatrists bumped into each other in the hospital cafeteria. "How am I feeling?" asked the first one of the second.

"Oh, just fine," said the second doctor. "How am *I* feeling?"

The secretary buzzed the doctor on the intercom and said, "there's a patient on the phone who wants to know if you make house calls—whatever *they* are!"

The man returned to the doctor's office to get the results of an extensive series of tests that were performed.

"Please sit down, Mr. Gilpin," the doctor said. "The tests are back and I'm afraid I've got some bad news."

"What's that, Doctor?"

"You've got cancer, Mr. Gilpin"

"Oh, that's terrible," Gilpin gasped and buried his face in his hands.

"And there's even worse news, I'm afraid, Mr. Gilpin. You've got Alzheimer's Disease."

"Well, at least I don't have cancer!"

"Hello, Mrs. Johnson. This is Dr. Olean calling. I'm calling with the results of your pregnancy test and I have some terrific news."

"My name is Miss Johnson, Doctor, and my boyfriend just ran off with another woman!"

There was a pause. "Well, in that case I'm calling with the results of your pregnancy test and I have some bad news!"

The young doctor came in to deliver the bad news. "I'm sorry, Mr. Jones, but you only have three minutes to live."

"Oh, that's terrible. Is there anything you can do?"

"Hmmm, let me think," said the doctor, rubbing his chin. "If I start right now, I might be able to boil you an egg!"

Mrs. Rush burst into the doctor's office. "Doctor! I am furious with you. My husband came to you two months ago with headaches. Since he saw you, he stays out late, never even comes home on the weekend, and hardly even looks at me anymore!"

The doctor was shocked. "I can't believe it! All I did was give him a new set of glasses!"

The doctor was on his way to a medical conference in Europe, and brought his secretary along to organize his appointments. Their plane arrived late and the two reached the hotel to find that they were assigned to just one room. Having to get up early the next day, they took it.

It was cold that night, as they both slipped under the covers. The secretary turned to the doctor. "Doctor, would you mind slipping out of bed to close the window?"

After a moment's hesitation, the doctor replied, "Would you like to pretend that you are my wife tonight?"

"Oh yes!" cried the secretary. "I was hoping you would ask me!"

"Good," said the doctor, turning over, "Then close the window yourself!"

A nervous woman went to the dentist.

"You know, Doctor, I hate having work done on my teeth. In fact, I think I would rather give birth than have a tooth drilled."

"That's up to you," the dentist replied. "But you'd better make up your mind before I adjust the chair!"

Brissie was having severe stomach pains and called his doctor for an appointment. The busy physician replied that he had no openings and he couldn't possibly see him for a month. In desperation, Brissie went to his pharmacist and begged for something to ease his discomfort. The following month, he arrived at the doctor's office at the appointed time.

"You know, Doctor," said Brissie, "the pharmacist gave me this blue concoction to take every three hours. She said to avoid physical activity and red meat. I've been doing it for four weeks but none of it did any good."

The doctor sniffed dismissively. "I know that pharmacist and she has a reputation for giving lousy advice. What else did she say?"

"She told me to come see you!"

Did you hear about the optometrist who fell into his lens grinder? He made a spectacle of himself.

Mr. Michaels went to the dentist to have a tooth removed. However, every time the dentist began to pull it out the patient would clamp his mouth shut. Trying to find a solution, the dentist took his assistant aside.

"The next time I reach for the tooth, I want you to take these forceps and give Mr. Michaels a big pinch in the side."

On his next attempt, the nurse administered a vicious pinch and Mr. Michael's mouth flew open. The tooth was extracted.

"Well, Mr. Michaels, that didn't hurt much, did it?" asked the doctor.

"Not too bad," commented Mr. Michaels. "But who would have thought the roots went so deep!"

The mark of a good doctor is usually illegible.
John Kelly

A nervous new father rushed into the hospital maternity ward where his wife had given birth. The doctor greeted him. "Mr. Jones, I think I should take you down to the nursery. I have something to show you."

"Doc, I am so nervous," blurted out the man.

"Don't worry, that's perfectly natural," assured the doctor.

Holding his hands over his eyes, the man said, "I don't think I can look!"

"I really think you ought to see this," said the doctor.

"Will you tell me what you see?" asked the man.

"Of course," assured the doctor.

"Is it a boy?"

The doctor hesitated. "The one in the middle is!"

A rich old woman, married and divorced many times, found another man willing to marry her despite her advancing years and past record. Before the wedding, she went to see her plastic surgeon, a trip she had often made before. When she told the doctor that she wanted yet another face-lift, he objected. "You've had at least ten face-lifts already. It would be both difficult and dangerous for you to have another, and I for one strongly recommend against it"

"Oh please, you must," the woman said. "I'm going to get married again, and to a much younger man. I can't walk down the aisle looking like this! Please!" But the doctor was unconvinced.

"All right," the woman said, "I'll throw in an extra ten thousand if you do it. I'm desperate." The doctor was suddenly moved with pity and decided to perform the operation.

After the operation, the woman admired her face in the mirror. "Doctor it looks marvelous! And it wasn't dangerous after all. One thing though," she said, fingering her chin, "I don't remember having a dimple. And it's so large!"

The doctor sighed. "I'm afraid it isn't a dimple at all. It's your navel!"

"Doctor! Doctor! I can't sleep at night!"

"Sleep during the day!"

An elderly couple went to the doctor. "What can I do for you?" the doctor asked.

"Doctor, we have a strange request. We'd like you to watch us make love."

Puzzled but willing, the doctor watched as the couple took off their clothes and began to have sex in his office. When they were through, they dressed and the doctor presented them with a bill for $15. "From what I observed," commented the doctor, "there is nothing wrong with the way in which you engage in sexual intercourse. In fact, I hope to have that much stamina at your age!"

"Thanks, Doctor," they both said as they left. They returned a week later and everything was repeated. This continued for a couple of weeks, at $15 a visit, until finally the doctor asked, "Look, I made it clear that there was nothing wrong with your technique. Why do you keep coming back?"

The man shyly answered, "It's like this. She's married so we can't go to her house. I'm married, so we can't meet at mine. The No-Tell Motel charges $27 for two hours. You only charge $15, and I get $8 back in Medicare!"

At the medical association meeting, the presiding doctor banged her gavel and said, "All in favor of the motion, stick out your tongue and say 'ah.'"

After two days in the hospital I took a turn for the nurse.

W. C. Fields

Did you hear about the hospital orderly who went into the army as a semi-private?

The two retired doctors were sitting in their beach chairs and watching the passing scene. One of them observed, "did you get a look at the great legs on that woman who just went by?"

"No, I didn't notice," replied the other. "I'm a chest man, you know."

The doctor finished his examination of the patient and was looking over the printouts of the various tests. "You say you feel rundown all the time, Mr. Hoyt, but your test results are all normal. Tell me, do you drink much alcohol?"

Mr. Hoyt shook his head. "Maybe a glass of wine occasionally, Doctor."

"Are you a smoker or does your wife smoke?"

Hoyt shook his head.

The doctor continued through a list of possible causes such as marital stress, problems at work, lack of exercise, and the like. To all of these questions, Hoyt shook his head.

Finally the doctor put down his clipboard. "Look, Mr. Hoyt, how am I going to cure you if you have nothing to give up?"

Anderson went to see a psychiatrist about some problems he was having. "What do you do for a living?" asked the psychiatrist.

"I'm an auto mechanic," he replied.

"Get under the couch."

An elderly patient hobbled into the doctor's office and collapsed in a chair. "Doctor, my right foot is giving me a lot of pain. Can you do something about it?"

The doctor shook his head. "Mr. Livingston, you'll just have to live with it. I'm afraid it's old age."

"Yeah? My left foot's not hurting me, and it's just as old."

Two nurses were having lunch in the hospital cafeteria. "Is Renata still dating that X ray technician?" asked the first.

"Yes," the second replied. "And I just don't understand it. The guy is so ugly and he has no personality."

"She must see something in him that others can't."

In the middle of the night, three laboratory test rats begin to talk.

"I'm very confused. I don't think I understand my psychologist," said the first.

"I think mine is kind of slow," said the second.

"I've got mine trained perfectly," said the third. "Every time I run through the maze, he has to feed me!"

Kearney went to the doctor for an examination. At the end of the exam the doctor looked up. "It is very serious. I afraid we must operate immediately."

"But, Doctor, I feel fine. This was just supposed to be a checkup!"

"I know, I know, these things are difficult to understand. It is also going to be expensive. It will cost $20,000."

Kearney was shocked. "Doctor, I don't have that kind of money!"

"We'll make it easy on you. I will operate now, and you can pay me back a little each month."

Kearney nodded. "Oh, kind of like you're buying a car!"

The doctor beamed. "I am!"

"The doctor is too frightened to see you."

A man went to his doctor for an examination. "I've lost my will to live, Doctor—except on the weekends."

The two young women were having lunch together.

"That psychiatrist I was working for was so critical she made my life a living hell," said the first.

"What did she do?"

"If I came in early, she told me I had an anxiety complex. If I came in late, I was being hostile. And if I came in on time I was being compulsive!"

"Doctor, what's the difference between an itch and an allergy?"

"About $50."

The young new intern was making his rounds in the psychiatric ward and came upon three patients standing in the hall. He peered at them for a moment and then consulted his charts. Then he turned to the first and asked, "How much is three times five?"

"Thursday," the man replied.

The doctor nodded and then asked the second patient, "How much is three times five?"

"January," the man said brightly.

Again the doctor nodded and turned to the last patient. "How much is three times five?"

"Fifteen."

The doctor raised his eyebrows. "And just how did you get that number?"

"Simple. I multiplied Thursday by January!"

An elderly man went to his doctor for a examination before his impending wedding with an older widow. All his tests were fine and his doctor pronounced him in good shape.

"One last test, Ben," said the doctor. "I'll need a semen sample. Take this small jar with you and bring me back a sample tomorrow or the next day."

Two days later Ben was back and handed the bottle to the doctor.

"It's empty, Ben," said the puzzled doctor.

"I know," sighed the elderly bachelor. "I'm really frustrated. I pulled it, I twisted it. My fiancée pulled it. She even put it in her mouth and bit on it."

"And what happened?" asked the doctor.

"Neither one of us could get the top of the jar off!"

A hypochondriac man went in to see a doctor. "Doctor, I've got the weirdest collection of symptoms," he said, not without some pride. "I'm sure my case is unique in the annals of medicine. What do you think I have?"

"Have you ever had these symptoms before?" asked the doctor.

"Yes."

"Well, you've got them again."

Q. How many doctors does it take to screw in a light bulb?

A. It all depends on the light bulb's health plan.

The surgeon motioned for his patient to sit down, "Mr. Palin, I've got the tests back and I'm afraid that an operation will be required. This is a very serious procedure and I have to tell you that three out of four patients don't survive this operation. But in your case, I wouldn't be concerned."

"Why is that, Doctor?"

"My last three patients died."

The leading banker in town went to the doctor for her annual checkup. The doctor x-rayed her, poked and prodded her, and checked her over thoroughly. Finally, the doctor was finished with his examination. "You're as sound as the dollar, Mrs. Benson."

Mrs. Benson turned white. "As bad as that, is it."

During the past year Ferris had been bothered with headaches and ringing in his ears. He had consulted numerous doctors and had tried any number of expensive remedies but nothing solved his problems. Finally he went to an old physician who diagnosed his malady.

"The problem is that you were never circumcised when you were an infant. The good news is that this is easily remedied. In fact, I can do it right here in the office."

Ferris was somewhat dubious, but since he had tried everything else, he reluctantly agreed. Minutes later the procedure was finished and the doctor presented him with a bill for $750.

"There you are, my good man. The headaches and ringing in your ears will soon be a thing of the past."

Ferris left in a upbeat mood and decided to buy a new fall suit to celebrate. He headed for a men's store across the street, where he was greeted at the door by a salesman.

"I want to get a new suit, shirt, tie, underwear, socks, and shoes. Everything," said Ferris. "I'm celebrating."

The salesman looked him up and down. "You've come to the right place, sir. I can see that you take a 42 suit jacket, 36 shorts, size 10½ shoes, size 12 socks, standard tie length, and a 16½-34 shirt.

Ferris shook his head. "You've got everything right but my collar size. I wear a 15½ instead of a 16½."

"I beg to differ, sir," the salesman demurred. "If you wore a 15½ collar, pretty soon you'd have headaches and ringing in your ears."

Before undergoing a surgical operation, arrange your temporal affairs. You may live.
Ambrose Bierce

William, a therapist in practice just a year, ran into one of his old classmates on the street. She asked how he was doing with his patients.

"It's really hard work," William sighed. "I am just exhausted after hearing clients tell me their problems for eight hours a day. But you look great. How do you look so fresh after a full day of listening to people tell you their neuroses?"

She smiled. "Who listens?"

Q. What's the difference between a psychiatrist and a psychologist?

A. A psychologist is a blind person in a completely dark attic looking for a black cat. A psychiatrist is a blind person in a completely dark attic looking for a black cat that isn't there.

There's no such thing as an unsuccessful operation. It's the recovery that gets 'em.
Lee Tully

A young intern was walking by the ward when she heard a patient call out to her. "Doctor, could you spare a moment?"

"Yes, Mrs. Allison, what is it?"

"Do you have the name of a good florist? I want to order some flowers for the head nurse."

"Oh, what a lovely idea. I'm sure she'll be very pleased to get them."

"Pleased?" snarled Mrs. Allison. "I've been ringing this darn buzzer for an hour with no response. I assumed she was dead!"

Two nurses were having a cup of coffee together. "Did you hear that Dr. Malachy has quit?" said the first. "He's giving up his practice."

"Malachy!" exclaimed the other. "But he's just in his forties. Why is he quitting?"

"Too many complaints about him. He had this habit of humming while he examined his patients."

"That doesn't seem so terrible."

"Ah, but he was humming 'Taps.'"

Did you ever notice how much a doctor's handwriting improves when it comes to writing out a bill?

Barry Mark

The doctor finished his examination of the patient and told him to get dressed. "I am afraid you are not in great shape, Ralph," admonished the doctor. "The best thing for you to do would be to give up liquor, cut out all that rich food at the fancy restaurants you've been going to, and stop dating all those young women who've been keeping you out late."

Ralph thought for a moment. "What's the next best thing?"

Three old classmates, one a surgeon, another an architect, and the third a politician, were having lunch together. They were arguing which of their professions was the oldest.

"Architecture is obviously the oldest," opined the architect. "Primitive humans needed a place to live and only an early architect could have brought order out of that chaos.

"Yes, but even before a structure could be built, physicians were needed to deliver babies and repair broken bones and bring some semblance of medicine to that primitive society. Clearly the physician is the oldest."

"Ah, my friends," said the politician. "I'm afraid that I have to agree that the architect came before the doctor and, yes, he did bring order out of chaos. But who do you think created the chaos in the first place?"

Sign on the door of the acupuncturist's office: "For a jab well done."

The two doctors met at a medical conference. "How's it going, Brad?" asked the first.

"Just fair, I'm afraid. Business is way down these past twelve months. I had a lot more patients last year."

"Really? What happened to them?"

Brad sighed, "They died."

Three surgeons were finishing their dinners at their exclusive club when the talk got around to their accomplishments. "My greatest challenge was a teenage tennis player who had his right arm cut off in an accident. I performed microsurgery to re-attach his muscles and arteries, and that young man is now the state tennis champion."

"All very well and good," said the second surgeon. "But last year I re-attached the hand of a young violinist who just won an international violin competition."

The third surgeon, who had been listening to the professional boasting, now leaned forward. "Both of you deserve all the credit in the world," he assured them. "But I've got you beat." The two surgeons looked at him in disbelief. "I performed extensive surgery on a cheat and a liar and gave him a winning smile and a firm handshake. Now he's our senator!"

"Did you hear that Dr. Hardaway has just written another new book?" said Anna to her friend.

"Well, I hope it's better than his other. In the last one he removed the appendix."

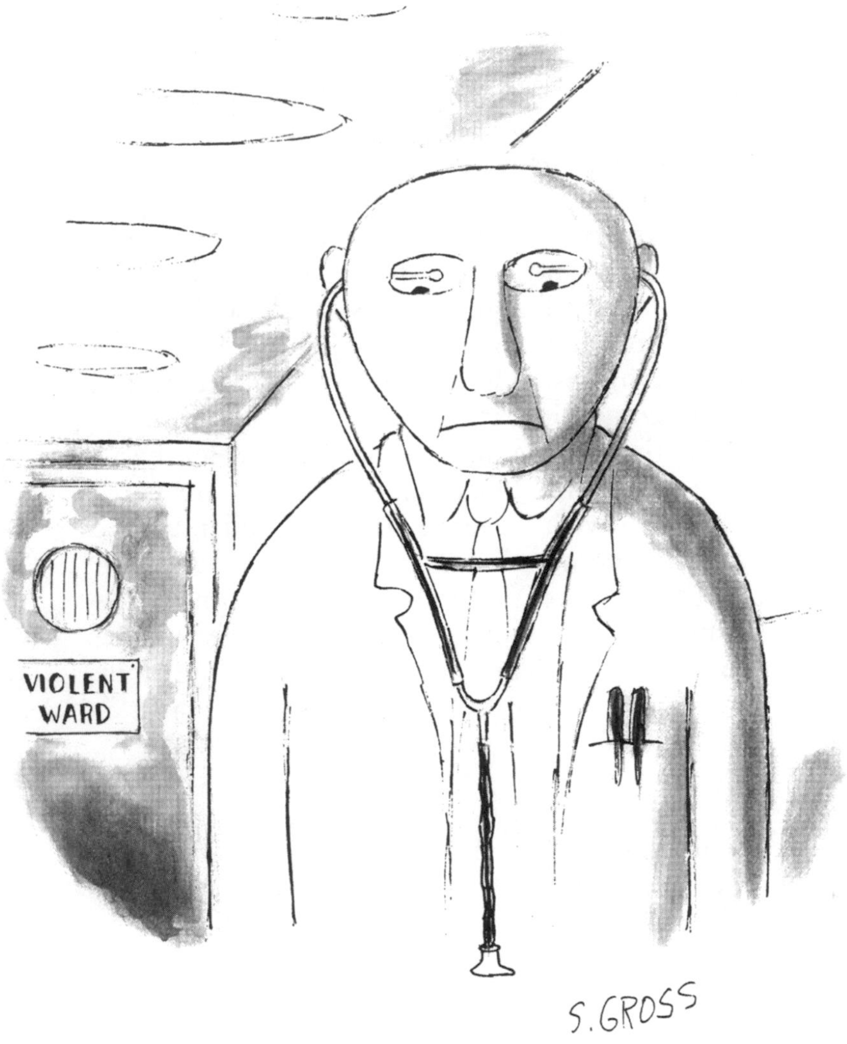
VIOLENT
WARD
S. GROSS

The doctor finished his examination as his patient, Mr. Twombly, struggled to pull his size 46 pants up over his large stomach. "Mr. Twombly, you've really gained some weight since your last physical exam," the doctor noted. "I'm putting you on this special diet." He handed the patient some xeroxed sheets with a diet spelled out. "Six months from now, I want to see two-thirds of you back in my office."

Schayes was a medical coroner who disliked all lawyers and stockbrokers, finding them greedy and opportunistic. Most of all, he hated trial lawyers, who always tried to twist his testimony in court. Reluctantly then, he agreed to appear in court in a case involving the large estate of deceased stockbroker. After Schayes was sworn in, the defense attorney approached him.

"Doctor, isn't it true that you didn't personally know the deceased, Mr. Alvin Rhoades?"

"That is true," answered Schayes.

"And isn't it true that you wouldn't recognize him if you met him?"

"Correct," acknowledged the doctor.

"And isn't it also correct that you don't even know whether my client is living or dead?" thundered the attorney.

"Oh yes, you're right there," replied Schayes quietly. "His brain is on a shelf at the morgue, but the rest of him may very well be out there somewhere selling junk bonds!"

After twelve years of therapy my psychiatrist said something that brought tears to my eyes. He said, "No hablo ingles."

Ronnie Shakes

A woman was leaving the dentist's office when a man walked in. She pointed to a sign that read "Painless Dentist" and mumbled, "It's not true."

"How do you know?" queried the new patient.

"Because he screamed when I bit his finger!"

Mark O'Donnell, a stockbroker, had been running a temperature for several days. Finally, he called his doctor and explained the situation.

After listening to the broker, the doctor prescribed, "Take some aspirin and that ought to relieve your symptoms. But if your temperature goes up a point or two, do you know what to do?"

"Yeah. Sell!"

Two men met on the street. "Hank, you don't look so good," offered the first man. "Is everything all right with you?"

Hank shook his head. "I don't know what it is, Ed. I just have no energy. Life is getting me down and I just mope through the day. I've been to different doctors, specialists, even a psychiatrist, but nothing seems to help."

Ed clucked sympathetically. "I'm sorry to hear that, buddy. Whenever I get feeling like that I just drag myself home, and then my wife gives me a great big hug, lays me down on the bed, and rubs my head and shoulders for an hour. Then I feel much better. You ought to try that."

"I think I will," agreed Hank. "What's your address?"

An attractive young woman was being shown around the ship by Tim, a young intern, who was explaining to her how he had gone through medical school on a Navy loan program. "And what is your specialty now?" asked the woman.

"I'm a naval surgeon," Tim responded.

"My, oh, my," sighed the woman. "Medicine is certainly getting specialized these days!"

Two mothers were having lunch and discussing their children and grandchildren. "How is young Marvin, the intern, doing?" asked Esther between mouthfuls.

"He's doing just fine," answered Nancy, "but he had to make a change from obstetrics to gynecology."

Esther raised her eyebrows, "He didn't like obstetrics?"

"Oh, he liked it fine," assured Nancy, "but apparently the part-time job he had in the post office while he was in medical school affected him."

"How could that job affect him?"

"He was delivering all the babies four weeks late!"

The doctor sat the 86-year-old man down for a talk.

"Congratulations on your upcoming wedding, Mr. Brower, but I thought it best to discuss a few things with you."

Mr. Brower leaned on his cane and peered at the doctor. "What's that, doctor?"

"Your fiancée is a lovely woman. She is 23 years old and in terrific shape." The doctor paused for a moment to consider his words. "Frankly speaking, she has had a very full sexual life, and after you two are married she expects to continue that way." The doctor sighed, "I'm just afraid this might be fatal."

Mr. Brower slammed his cane on the desk. "If she dies, she dies!"

"Doctor, I feel run down and exhausted all the time," complained the patient. "I am totally listless. Is there anything you can give me that will perk me up?"

"Yes. Wait till you get my bill."

A doctor called one of his patients. "Mr. Thompson, your check came back."

"So did my lumbago!"

A sign in the emergency ward:
Interns think of God.
Residents pray to God.
Doctors believe they're God.
Nurses are God.

"I think I know one problem you've got," said the psychiatrist to her patient. "You have trouble making up your mind. Would you agree with that?"

"Well, yes and no."

Hilda walked into the hospital ward and sat down next to her sister's bed. "Here, Martha, I brought you some flowers, a book, and plenty of gossip to tell you about."

"Great!" said Martha, who sat up and pressed the buzzer for the nurse.

Her sister was mystified. "Why did you ring for the nurse now?"

"To make sure we aren't interrupted for a half hour."

"I'm sorry to have kept you waiting all afternoon, but we've been really busy," said the doctor showing the patient into his office.

"That's perfectly all right, doctor. But it might have been better if you'd seen my ailment in it's early stages!"

A long-haired disc jockey went to the doctor's office for his yearly examination. The doctor looked him all over and then started to listen to the patient's heart through a stethoscope. He continued to listen as he moved the stethoscope around to different positions.

"What's the matter, Doc?" asked the patient. "Can't find a station you like?"

Violet went to the hospital to visit her friend, Roberta, who was recovering from her sixth operation in four years. Much to Violet's surprise, she found Roberta sitting up in bed eating her lunch and watching television.

"You look awfully good for someone who's just recovering from another operation," Voilet gushed. "I expected you to be flat on your back and barely able to communicate, but you look great."

Roberta smiled. "Yes, it was much easier this time than when I was here eight months ago. It went faster and smoother."

"Really? How come?" asked Violet.

"After the last operation, they put in zippers."

Doctors and lawyers must go to school for years, often with little sleep and with great sacrifice to their first wives.

Roy Blount, Jr.

"There is a marvelous new drug just out that I want you to try, Mrs. Shackleford," said the doctor handing her a prescription.

"Thank you, doctor," Mrs. Shackleford replied. "But tell me, if I take these for a long time, will there be any side effects?"

"Yes. Bankruptcy!"

A snail was crossing a road when a turtle came along and ran him over. The snail woke up in the emergency room. "What happened?" asked the attending doctor.

"I really don't know," gasped the snail. "It happened so fast."

She got her looks from her father. He's a plastic surgeon.

Groucho Marx

Two friends, Bill and Ray, who had not seen each other in many years met for a drink. In the interim, Ray had undergone a sex change operation and was filling Bill in on the details. "Is there anything you miss now that you're a woman?" asked Bill.

"I just wish I could remember how to parallel park."

I know that the issue of health care concerns everyone. I saw a little boy and girl playing doctor: she asked what HMO he belonged to.

"Doctor! Doctor. I think I have amnesia."
"Go home and forget about it."

The patient lay on the psychiatrist's couch. "Doctor, I just can't get to sleep at night," he complained.
"Why is that?"
"I am trying to solve all the world's problems."
"That's a tall order. Any success?" asked the psychiatrist.
"Oh, I get most of the problems solved."
"Then what's the problem?"
"It's those damn ticker tape parades in my honor that keep me awake."

Did you hear about the dentist who married a manicurist? Now they fight tooth and nail.

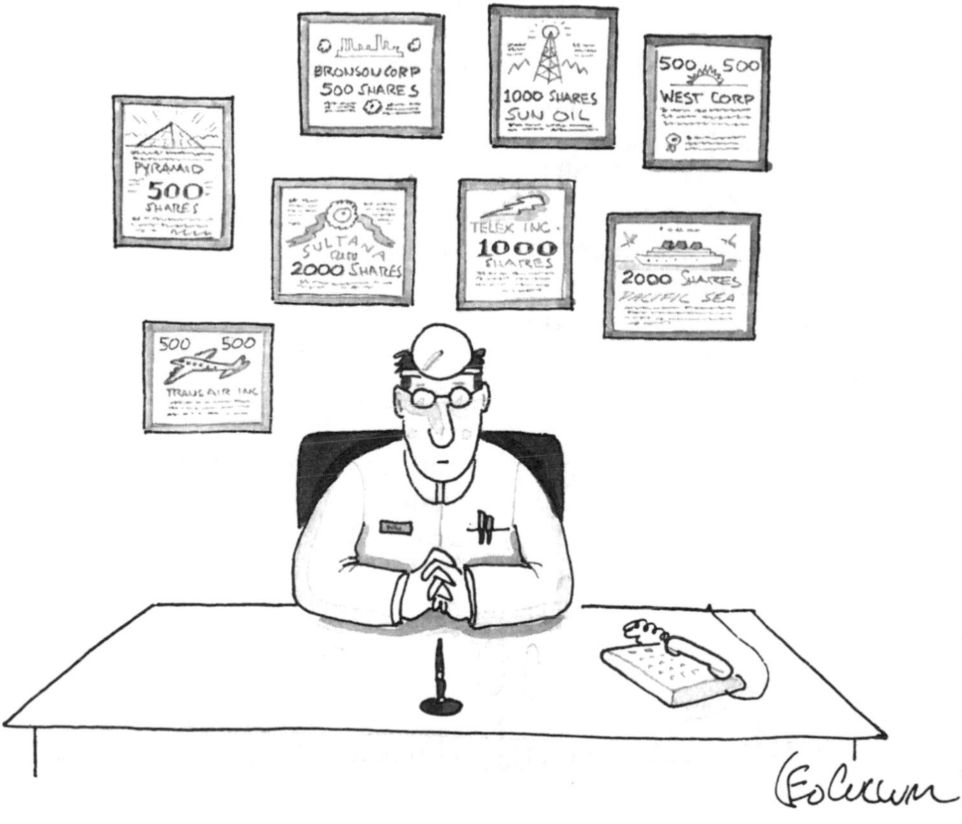
BRONSONCORP
500 SHARES
1000 SHARES
SUN OIL
500 500
WEST CORP
PYRAMID
500
SHARES
SULTANA
2000 SHARES
TELEX INC.
1000
SHARES
2000 SHARES
PACIFIC SEA
500 500
TRANS AIR INC

A prominent doctor died and arrived at the Pearly Gates where he was ushered in to meet God. "You've led an exemplary life, Doctor," God intoned. "You may ask one question of me."

The doctor thought for a minute, then brightened. "Will there be health care reform?"

God sighed. "There's some good news and some bad news. The good news is yes, there will be health care reform."

"And the bad news?"

"Not in *my* lifetime."

"Doctor, I'm worried about my husband. His mind seems to be wandering."

"Don't worry, Mrs. Nordstrom. I know your husband. It won't get far."

A patient in the hospital was complaining to the nurse. "I hate this place. They treat us like dogs."

"That's not true. Now roll over."

An 85-year-old man, recently married to a woman in her twenties, went to the doctor for a physical. As the doctor was finishing the series of examinations, the man announced proudly, "Did you hear that my wife is pregnant?"

The doctor didn't say anything, and the man repeated his question.

"I'm reminded of the story of the absent-minded hunter," the doctor answered. "He was going out to hunt for bear and instead of his gun, he absentmindedly picked up an umbrella. When he spotted a bear, the animal charged towards him. The hunter pointed the umbrella at the bear, shot, and killed him."

The patient thought for a moment. "That's impossible. There must have been another hunter on the other side."

"Exactly."

A doctor and his wife were arguing. "And another thing," the doctor yelled, "you're terrible in bed." With that, he slammed out of the house and went to his office. A few hours later, however, he was feeling contrite and called his wife to apologize. The phone rang for a long time before his wife picked it up.

"Where were you?" he demanded.

"I was in bed," was the reply.

"What were you doing in bed in the middle of the day?"

"Getting a second opinion."

Chloe was afraid of dentists and had not been to see one in years. After much arguing, her husband convinced her to go, and together they visited the dentist's office. After examining Chloe's teeth, the dentist turned to the husband and remarked, "Your wife has a terrible bite."

"You think that's bad, you ought to hear her bark."

"The doctor told me to lose some weight, so I joined a health club," said Marilyn.

"Did it work?"

"Yes, I now weigh $1,500 less."

Sign in the obstetrics ward of the hospital: "Research shows that the first five minutes of life can be the most risky."

Underneath someone had scrawled: "The last five minutes aren't so great either."

Jody was telling her friends about how the first aid course that she completed had prepared her for an emergency earlier in the day.

"I saw this accident where a pedestrian was hit by a car. His arm and one of his legs was broken. His nose was to the side of his face and he was covered with blood."

"So what did you do?" asked her friend.

"Thanks to the first aid course, I knew exactly what to do. I sat down on the curb and put my head between my knees to keep from fainting!"

The psychiatrist turned to her patient and shook his hand. "In my profession we rarely tell a patient that he or she is cured, but after six years of therapy, Mr. Smedley, I am saying to you that you are a cured man."

Smedley just frowned.

"Why aren't you happy about this?" asked
the psychiatrist.
"Six years ago I was Napoleon Bonaparte.
Now I'm nobody."

"Doctor, you've got to examine my husband,"
pleaded Mrs. Kearney. "He thinks he's the Lone
Ranger."
"Has this been going on for long?"
"Five years."
"Don't worry," assured the doctor. "Bring
him in and I'll cure him."
"I guess that's what I want," murmured Mrs.
Kearney. "But, then again, Tonto's so good
with the children."

I've always been a hypochondriac. As a little
boy, I'd eat my M&Ms with a glass of water.
Richard Lewis

Bonnie was scheduled to talk to 2,000 delegates
at a national convention the following day,
when she was struck by acute stomach pains.
She was rushed to the hospital where her family physician performed emergency stomach

THE DOCTOR JOKE BOOK

surgery. When he cut her open, a flock of butterflies flew out.

"Well, I'll be," marveled the doctor. "she *was* telling the truth."

"Do you think you'll be able to afford five sessions a week?" asked the psychiatrist.

"Don't worry, Doc. I'll pay or my name isn't Attila the Hun."

The Kansas farmer went to see his doctor. "You've got to give me something for my sneezing," the farmer wheezed.

After looking the farmer over, the doctor said, "The best thing for you would be three weeks in Arizona."

The farmer shook his head. "Oh, I can't do that. I've got 2,500 acres of ragweed to harvest."

A husband and wife went to the doctor for a yearly checkup. The husband was ushered in first, and after the doctor had completed his tests, he asked him if he had any particular concerns.

"One thing has been bothering me, doctor— our love making. The first time was fine, but

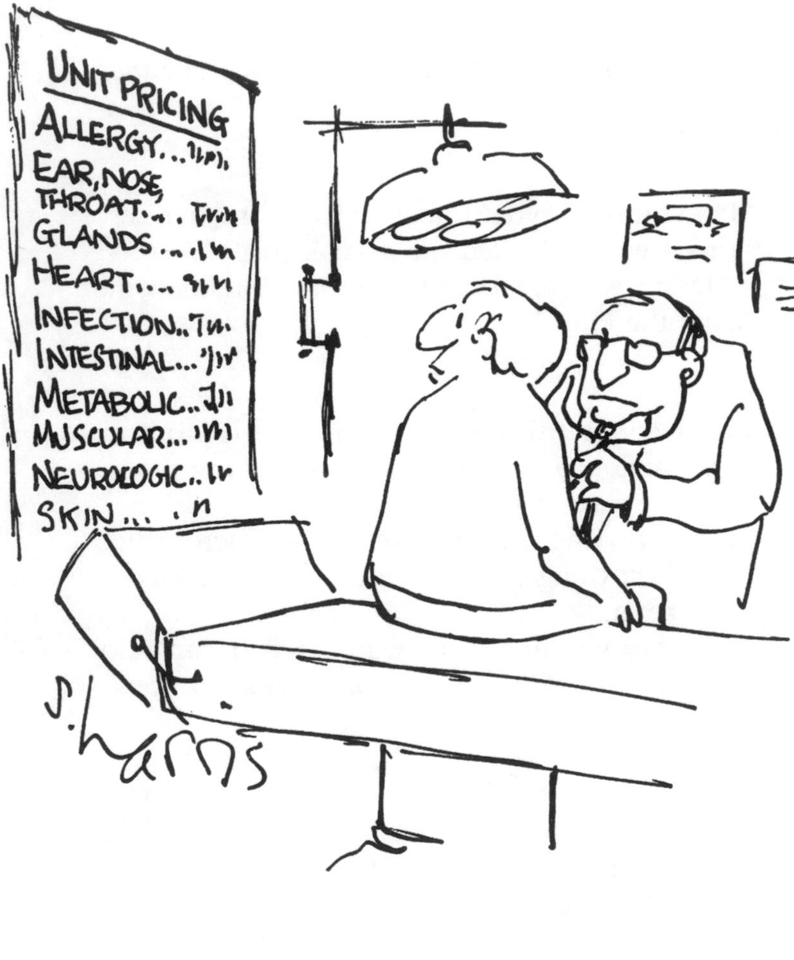
UNIT PRICING
ALLERGY...
EAR, NOSE, THROAT....
GLANDS...
HEART....
INFECTION..
INTESTINAL...
METABOLIC..
MUSCULAR...
NEUROLOGIC..
SKIN...
S. Harris

the second time I noticed that I was sweating all over."

The doctor was perplexed, and went in to see the wife in another examining room. "Your husband says that the first time he made love he was fine, but that he was sweating all over the second time. Do you know why?"

"I certainly do," snapped the wife. "The first time was January and the second time was August."

Phil went to his dentist for a yearly checkup. After a thorough examination, the doctor said, "I've got some good news and some bad news."

"What's the good news?"

"The good news is that my son is going to Columbia Medical School."

"What's the bad news?"

"You're paying for it."

The doctor and his family were on vacation in Florida. They were strolling along the beach when the doctor spotted a fin in the water and keeled over in a dead faint. Reviving a few minutes later, he looked up at his wife. "It's okay, Harold," she said sympathetically. "But you've got to stop imagining that you see lawyers everywhere."

One nurse to another: "What do you give a man who has everything?"
"Penicillin!"

A car ran through a stop sign at an intersection and rammed into the side of another car. The errant driver quickly rushed over to the disabled vehicle and saw that the driver's door was open and the driver was sprawled on the pavement.
"Are you all right?" the first driver asked, observing that the man was slowly getting to his feet and brushing off his clothes.
"How should I know?" retorted the angry driver. "I'm a doctor, not a lawyer."

"Doctor, I've decided I should get a vasectomy," said the middle-aged patient.
"This is a very serious step, Mr. Bowton," said the doctor, "have you discussed this with your children?"
"Yes, I have. They voted 13 to 2 in favor!"

"I hear Dr. Rogers and Dr. McCord aren't sharing office space anymore," said one nurse to another. "What happened?"

"It's terrible," sighed the other. "Rogers was trying to steal patients, and McCord is now suing him for alienation of infections!"

There's another advantage of being poor—a doctor will cure you faster.

Kin Hubbard

An elderly man constantly called his doctor at all hours of the day and night and would then keep her on the phone with a litany of imagined ailments. Finally the doctor could take it no longer.

"Listen, Mr. Becker. If you wake me up again in the middle of the night with another one of your tales about some made-up ailment, I am going to insist you go to another physician. Have I made myself clear?" And she hung up the phone.

A week later, the unfortunate man slipped and fell down a flight of stairs, breaking his hip, two ribs, an elbow, and suffering a concussion. He was rushed to the hospital and put in intensive care. An hour later, his doctor walked in on him, saw his condition, and beamed, "Now I think you're getting the hang of it!"

Suggested slogan of the American Dental Association: Nothing dentured, nothing gained.

A formidable-looking woman stomped into the dentist's office and announced,"I would like a tooth pulled. I would like it done immediately. And since I am in a hurry, I do not want any anesthetics or drugs used."

The dentist was impressed with her bravery. "Where is the tooth?" he asked.

The woman turned to a young boy behind her. "Dennis, show him your tooth."

Doctors are men who prescribe medicine of which they know little to cure diseases of which they know less in human beings of which they know nothing.
Voltaire

"Mrs. Elway, you were supposed to lose weight," said the doctor. "According to the scale here, you've gained twenty pounds since we last saw you. What happened to your diet?

"To tell you the truth, Doctor. I haven't been on a diet in a month of sundaes."

Two Iowa farmers were sitting in a diner having coffee and chatting about the day's events. "Says here in the paper, Clem, that in New York City one woman is run over by a car every five minutes."

"Really? I hope she has a good health plan."

A woman ran out of her building and hailed a cab. "Quick. The maternity ward at City Hospital," she screeched. Seeing the stricken look on the cabbie's face, she added, "Don't worry, pal. I'm just late for work."

An elderly man hobbled into the doctor's waiting room and collapsed in a chair next to the only other patient, a white-haired but alert-looking gentleman. "Whatcha here for?" rasped the new arrival.

"Just a general checkup," the other man replied.

"Well, you look pretty good to me. What's your secret?"

"No secret. I drink a quart of bourbon a day, smoke about two cartons of cigarettes, and I'm usually out late every night with at least one young woman."

"That's amazing," marveled the other. "How old are you?"

"Twenty-four."

Doctor Zizzner finished with his examination of his eighty-year-old patient. "You're in perfect health for a woman your age, Mrs. Habib. Is there anything else you need?"

"I'd like some birth control pills, doctor."

"Really, Mrs. Habib, I don't think those are necessary."

"You don't understand, Doctor. They're for my headache."

The doctor chuckled. "Mrs. Habib, birth control pills won't cure a headache."

"Oh, yes they will. I put them in my granddaughter's coffee and my headache goes away."

The nurse was walking from the hospital when she spotted a man lying face down in the gutter. She rushed over to him, quickly turned him over, and started mouth-to-mouth resuscitation. After a few seconds, the man began sputtering and flailing his arms. Then he sat up. "Lady, do you mind? I'm trying to clean the gutter."

Doctor Johnson was having lunch in the hospital cafeteria when he was joined by a colleague. "I know you've been avoiding me, Johnson, and I also know you are having an affair with my wife."

"It is true," admitted Dr. Johnson.

"So, how is she in bed?" asked the colleague.

"What a question to ask," replied the astonished doctor. "You should know, you're married to her."

"Yeah. But I wanted a second opinion."

Did you hear about the doctor who spent every last cent he had on gambling? In a desperate attempt to pay off his gambling debts, he decided to rob a bank. But the teller couldn't read his note!

Bennett Cerf

The phone rang in Dr. Watterman's home just as the physician was taking off his coat. He answered the call, listened for a moment, and then slammed the phone down. "Quick, get me my medical kit and the car keys. There's a man on the phone who says he can't live without me."

Watterman's daughter rolled her eyes. "Daddy, I believe that call was for me."

A man walked into a psychiatrist's office and started pacing up and down. "What seems to be the matter?" asked the doctor.

"I'm not sure what my problem is, Doctor. One minute I think I'm a teepee, the next minute I think I'm a wigwam. Then I think I'm a teepee again."

"Just sit down and relax," said the doctor. "You're two tents."

A woman in her mid forties walked into her doctor's office. Blushing a little, she began haltingly, "Doctor, I'm having some difficulty."

The doctor, sensing something was bothering the woman, replied, "Please Mrs. Hoffman, I'm a doctor. I'm sure I've heard far worse then you can tell me."

The woman continued. "Well, it started a few days ago. I went to the bathroom, and to my shock, pennies started coming out. I didn't really worry. I figured it would stop."

"I understand. Go on," the doctor encouraged.

"To my surprise, when I went to the bathroom the next day, nickels starting coming out. This was even more uncomfortable and upsetting."

"Of course it was," nodded the doctor.

"On Thursday, I went to the bathroom, and out came a bunch of shiny dimes. At this point, I was afraid of what would happen the next day."

"And just what did happen?" asked the doctor.

"As I feared, today quarters came out. Doctor, what do you make of all this?"

The doctor smiled gently at the woman. "It's no problem, Mrs. Hoffman. You're just going through the change."

Show me the father of our country's dentures, and I'll show you the George Washington Bridge.

Soupy Sales

An elderly woman named Emma was visiting her friend in a nursing home. "It was a terrible blow," sighed Emma. "Jake's health was failing and the doctor prescribed these ten very expensive pills for him take. He had taken just five of them when the dear man passed away." Emma shook her head and dabbed her eyes.

Her friend reached over, grasped her hand, and said consolingly, "Ah, it is terrible. But just think what might've happened if he had taken all ten!"

"That's quite a nurse you've got there, Doctor," said the young patient in his twenties pointing to a good-looking redheaded woman in white. "Why, just one touch of her hand miraculously cured my fever."

"Yes, I know," sighed the doctor. "I could hear her slap all the way down the hall."

A young doctor inquired of an older colleague, "Why do you always ask your patients what they've had for dinner?"

"It is very simple. I make out the bill according to the dinner menu!"

Two or three times a week, it was the usual practice of the eminent surgeon, Dr. Madjian, to finish an exhausting eight-hour session in the operating room with a daiquiri at a neighboring bar. This was one of those days, and the tired doctor sat down at the end of the bar and waved to the bartender for a drink. A minute later, the bartender slid the doctor's drink in front of him. He raised it to his lips, took a sip, and then made a wry face. "Henry, what did you put in this? This isn't my usual."

The sheepish bartender spread his hands. "I'm sorry. I ran out of limes and so I substituted ground hickory nuts. It's a hickory daiquiri, Doc!"

Thanks to jogging, more people are collapsing in perfect health than ever before.
Sunshine Magazine

The hypochondriac walked into the doctor's office and sat down. "Well, what is it this week, Mr. Wells. What ailment do you have for me?"

"That's just it, Doctor, I don't know. My subscription to the *New England Journal of Medicine* ran out."

A Frenchman, an Englishman, and an Israeli were working on an atomic power plant in the middle of the desert when they were accidentally exposed to a lethal dosage of radiation. A doctor examined them and sadly shook her head. "The three of you have been exposed to a kajillahertz of lethal radiation which is invariably fatal. You have at best just four months to live," sighed the doctor. "But since it was a government project you were working on, and we want to make your final moments as pleasant as possible, I am authorized to grant you, within reason, one last wish."

The Frenchman stepped forward first. "I wish to spend my last night with the most beautiful woman in the world." The doctor nodded to her assistant who jotted down the request.

The Englishman spoke next. "I would like an audience with her majesty, Queen Elizabeth, before I die." The doctor nodded and thought that could be arranged.

The Israeli then stepped forward. "I want to see another doctor."

Californians are so health conscious. They think it's bad luck to spill salt substitute.
Johnny Carson

ANGRY BIRDS™
FLIGHT SCHOOL

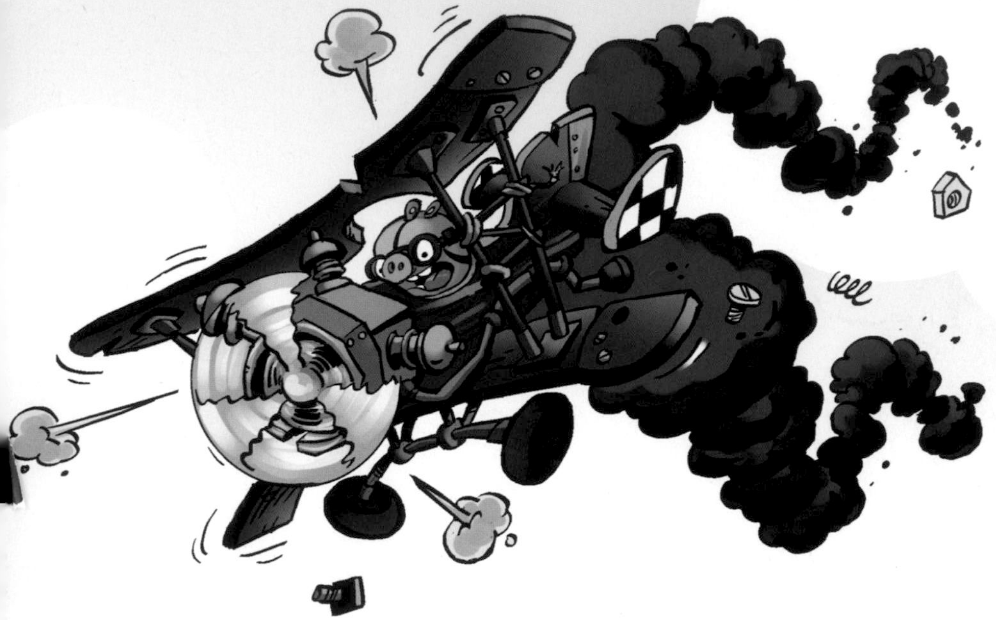

COVER ARTWORK BY: PHILIP MURPHY
EDITED FOR IDW BY: DAVID HEDGECOCK
EDITORIAL ASSISTANCE BY: DAVID MARIOTTE AND CHASE MAROTZ
COLLECTION EDITS BY: JUSTIN EISINGER & ALONZO SIMON
COLLECTION PRODUCTION BY: SHAWN LEE
PUBLISHER: TED ADAMS

KAIKEN
PUBLISHING LTD.

Mikael Hed, Chairman of the Board
Laura Nevanlinna, Publishing Director
Jukka Heiskanen, Editor-in-Chief, Comics
Juha Mäkinen, Editor, Comics
Perhi Haikonen, AD
Nathan Cosby, Freelance Editor

ROVIO

Thanks to Jukka Heiskanen, Juha Mäkinen and the Kaiken team for their hard work and invaluable assistance.

For international rights, contact licensing@idwpublishing.com

ISBN: 978-1-68405-001-7

20 19 18 17   1 2 3 4

IDW
www.IDWPUBLISHING.com

Ted Adams, CEO & Publisher • Greg Goldstein, President & COO • Robbie Robbins, EVP/Sr. Graphic Artist • Chris Ryall, Chief Creative Officer •
David Hedgecock, Editor-in-Chief • Laurie Windrow, Senior Vice President of Sales & Marketing • Matthew Ruzicka, CPA, Chief Financial Officer •
Lorelei Bunjes, VP of Digital Services • Jerry Bennington, VP of New Product Development

Facebook: facebook.com/idwpublishing • Twitter: @idwpublishing • YouTube: youtube.com/idwpublishing
Tumblr: tumblr.idwpublishing.com • Instagram: instagram.com/idwpublishing

RED IN...

YOU GOT IT BACKWARDS

ANGRY BIRDS

ABM 2015-007

YOUR HAT'S ON *BACKWARDS,* DUMMY.

HEY!!!

WATCH WHERE YOU'RE *GOING!*

WHOOOSHH

HEY BUDDY! *HERE!* HAVE A COUPLE DOLLARS!

HUH?

WHAT'S GOING ON?

WRITTEN BY: **PAUL TOBIN** • ART & COLORS BY: **CORRADO MASTANTUONO** • LETTERS BY: **PISARA OY**

3

OH.

GREAT! ANOTHER HOLIDAY. JUST WHAT I NEED. IT'S AS BAD AS *BE NICE DAY*, OR *TALK LIKE A PIRATE DAY*, OR *WEAR TWO HATS DAY*, OR *EAT BREAKFAST FOUR TIMES DAY*...

...OR *SNEEZE LIKE A PIRATE DAY*, OR *DRAW A CAT ON YOUR FOREHEAD DAY*, OR *SMELL LIKE A PIRATE DAY*.

ARRGHH!

ALL THESE *HOLIDAYS!*

I *HATE* THEM!

WHY DO *I* ALWAYS HAVE TO CELEBRATE?

WHY DO THESE THINGS KEEP *INTERFERING* IN MY LIFE?

I HATE HOLIDAYS!

4

CLAPCLAPCLAPCLAPCL

WOW! YOU MUST *REALLY* LOVE BACKWARDS DAY.

UMM, WHAT?

WELL, IT'S BACKWARDS DAY! SO YOU'RE SAYING THINGS BACKWARDS, RIGHT?

AND, SINCE YOU'RE SAYING YOU *HATE* BACKWARDS DAY...

BACKWARD DAY

...YOU MUST *LOVE* IT!

NO. I... HATE IT?

HA! SEE! HE *LOVES* IT!

AND SOON...

YOU SHOULD GROOM YOURSELF BETTER. YOU LOOK LIKE AN IDIOT.

THANKS, MISTER!

I'M TAKING THIS CAKE. SO... SINCE IT'S BACKWARDS DAY... YOU OWE *ME* FIVE DOLLARS.

THAT'S THE SPIRIT!

ALL CAKES 5$ EACH

YOUR TASTE IN MUSIC IS *TERRIBLE*.

THANK YOU. MUCH APPRECIATED!

I DON'T LIKE YOU!

AWW, THAT TRULY WARMS MY HEART!

THAT HAT LOOKS LIKE A PILE OF EXPLODED PANCAKES.

OH! YOU *LIKE* IT? I DESIGNED IT MYSELF!

GEE. RED IS USUALLY KIND OF MEAN, BUT HERE ON BACKWARDS DAY, HE'S... NICE.

YEAH. YOU'RE RIGHT!

YAYY! RED!

HURRAH!

WHAT A GREAT GUY!

HUHH?

THANK YOU! I, UHH... LIKE YOU GUYS TOO.

HUH?

UMM. I MEAN... YOU GUYS ARE ALL JERKS!

I DON'T LIKE A SINGLE ONE OF YOU!

YAYYY!

HMMM, I COULD GET USED TO THIS.

IT'S... NICE TO HAVE FRIENDS.

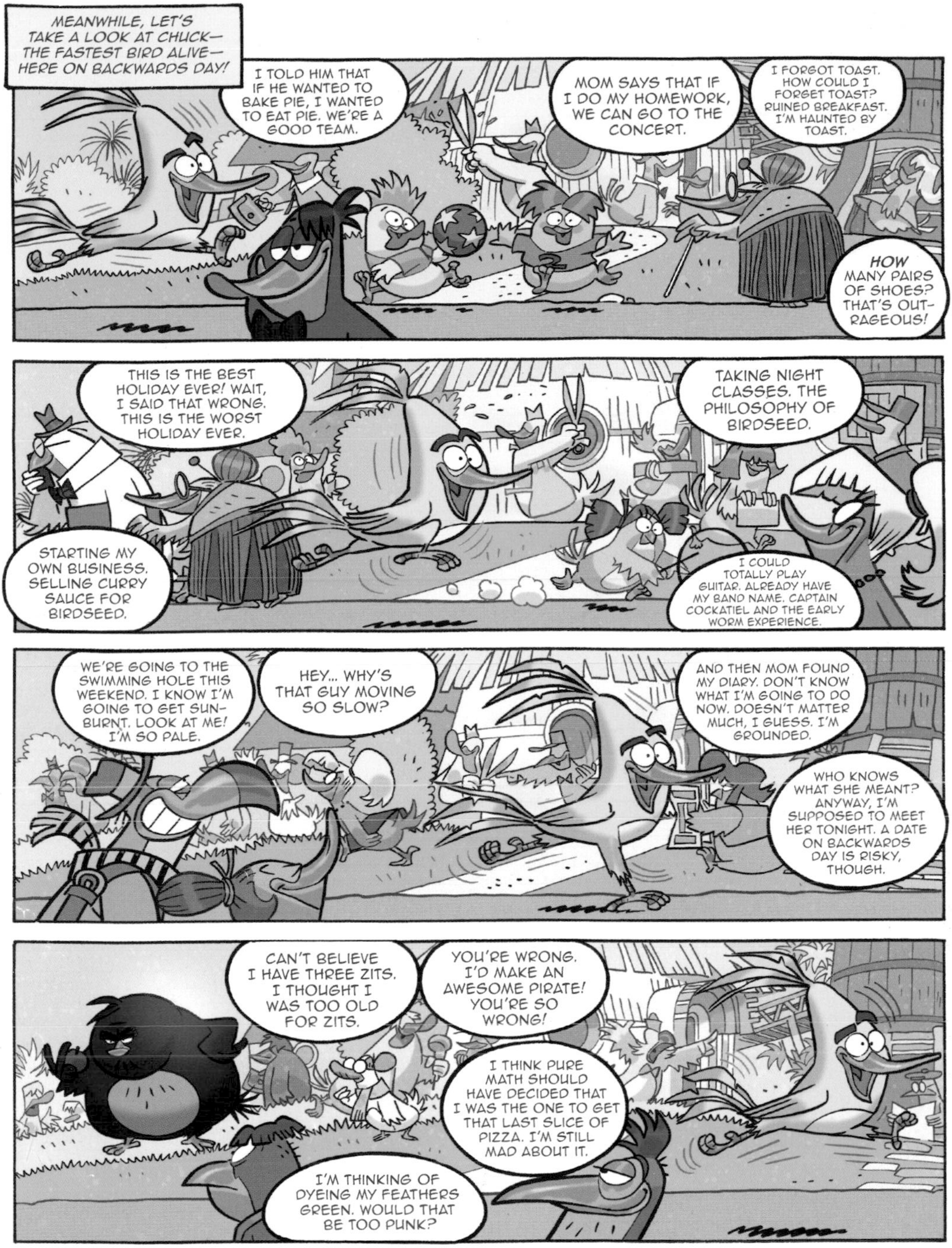
MEANWHILE, LET'S TAKE A LOOK AT CHUCK—THE FASTEST BIRD ALIVE—HERE ON BACKWARDS DAY!
I TOLD HIM THAT IF HE WANTED TO BAKE PIE, I WANTED TO EAT PIE. WE'RE A GOOD TEAM.
MOM SAYS THAT IF I DO MY HOMEWORK, WE CAN GO TO THE CONCERT.
I FORGOT TOAST. HOW COULD I FORGET TOAST? RUINED BREAKFAST. I'M HAUNTED BY TOAST.
HOW MANY PAIRS OF SHOES? THAT'S OUTRAGEOUS!
THIS IS THE BEST HOLIDAY EVER! WAIT, I SAID THAT WRONG. THIS IS THE WORST HOLIDAY EVER.
TAKING NIGHT CLASSES. THE PHILOSOPHY OF BIRDSEED.
STARTING MY OWN BUSINESS. SELLING CURRY SAUCE FOR BIRDSEED.
I COULD TOTALLY PLAY GUITAR. ALREADY HAVE MY BAND NAME. CAPTAIN COCKATIEL AND THE EARLY WORM EXPERIENCE.
WE'RE GOING TO THE SWIMMING HOLE THIS WEEKEND. I KNOW I'M GOING TO GET SUNBURNT. LOOK AT ME! I'M SO PALE.
HEY... WHY'S THAT GUY MOVING SO SLOW?
AND THEN MOM FOUND MY DIARY. DON'T KNOW WHAT I'M GOING TO DO NOW. DOESN'T MATTER MUCH, I GUESS. I'M GROUNDED.
WHO KNOWS WHAT SHE MEANT? ANYWAY, I'M SUPPOSED TO MEET HER TONIGHT. A DATE ON BACKWARDS DAY IS RISKY, THOUGH.
CAN'T BELIEVE I HAVE THREE ZITS. I THOUGHT I WAS TOO OLD FOR ZITS.
YOU'RE WRONG. I'D MAKE AN AWESOME PIRATE! YOU'RE SO WRONG!
I THINK PURE MATH SHOULD HAVE DECIDED THAT I WAS THE ONE TO GET THAT LAST SLICE OF PIZZA. I'M STILL MAD ABOUT IT.
I'M THINKING OF DYEING MY FEATHERS GREEN. WOULD THAT BE TOO PUNK?

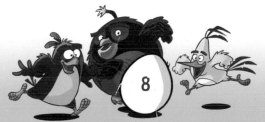

AND HOW IS TERENCE—THE STRONGEST BIRD IN THE WORLD—CELEBRATING BACKWARDS DAY?

DROP

URGG.

UGHH! GNNNNNNN

NEED *HELP,* SONNY?

NAB

F!!!

AND THEN...

I HOPE EVERYONE HAS HAD A GOOD... ERR, I MEAN *ROTTEN*... TIME TODAY!

AND NOW, IT'S TIME TO COUNT THE VOTE TOTALS FOR THE *BEST GUY OF BACKWARDS DAY* AWARD!

celebrate BACKWARDS DAY

WOOOO! IT WAS ANOTHER *CLOSE* CONTEST THIS YEAR, FOLKS! WHO'S GOING TO WIN?

LET'S SEE... ALMOST EVERYONE IN TOWN VOTED, AND... LOOKS LIKE...

WINNER

...*RED* IS THE *ONLY* PERSON IN TOWN WHO GOT *NO* VOTES! ZERO! NOT A *SINGLE SOLITARY* VOTE FOR BEST GUY OF BACKWARDS DAY!

AND OF COURSE THAT MEANS...

HE WINS!

WHAT? OH! OH YEAH! IT'S BACKWARDS DAY!

AND I GOT *NO* VOTES! ME! WOW!

CLAP
CLAP
CLAP

10

NOW, NORMALLY, WHEN YOU WIN A GRAND PRIZE, WE GIVE OUT THINGS LIKE... *THIS TROPHY!*

OR POTS FILLED WITH *MONEY!*

OR MAYBE DATES WITH CELEBRITIES, LIKE VIVETTE VA VA VOOM!

BUT SINCE THIS IS *BACKWARDS DAY,* WE WANTED THE AWARD TO BE A LITTLE SOMETHING *DIFFERENT,* SO *YOU* GET....

...TO CLEAN UP AFTER THE PARADE!

YAY, RED!
YOU'RE THE
BEST!

HEY.

12

THE GARDEN

ANGRY BIRDS™

Written by: PAUL TOBIN • Art & colors by: DIANE FAYOLLE • Letters by: PISARA OY

BOMB, IT'S BEEN SEVEN HOURS SINCE SHE LEFT. MAYBE YOU SHOULD CHECK IN ON THE FLOWERS?

HMMM. LOOK AT ALL THESE BEES ON THE FLOWERS!

I NEED TO GET RID OF THEM.

GO AWAY! GET OUT OF HERE!

GO AWAY!

KEEP OFF THE FLOWERS!

SHOOO!!

GO AWAY!

?

BZZZZ

KEEP OFF THE FLOWERS!

HAAA!! OUCH!

STING

GAHH!

STING! STING

AND SO...

TOOK THREE HOURS AND ABOUT THREE HUNDRED BEE-STINGS, BUT I MANAGED TO CHASE ALL THE BEES AWAY!

BEES ARE ACTUALLY GOOD FOR FLOWERS.

OH.

TAP TAP

AND SO...

GO THAT WAY! THAT WAY!

COME BACK!

I'M SORRY!!

BZZZZ

OUCH!

ALL BEES ARE WELCOME

BZZZ

TO THE FLOWERS!

14

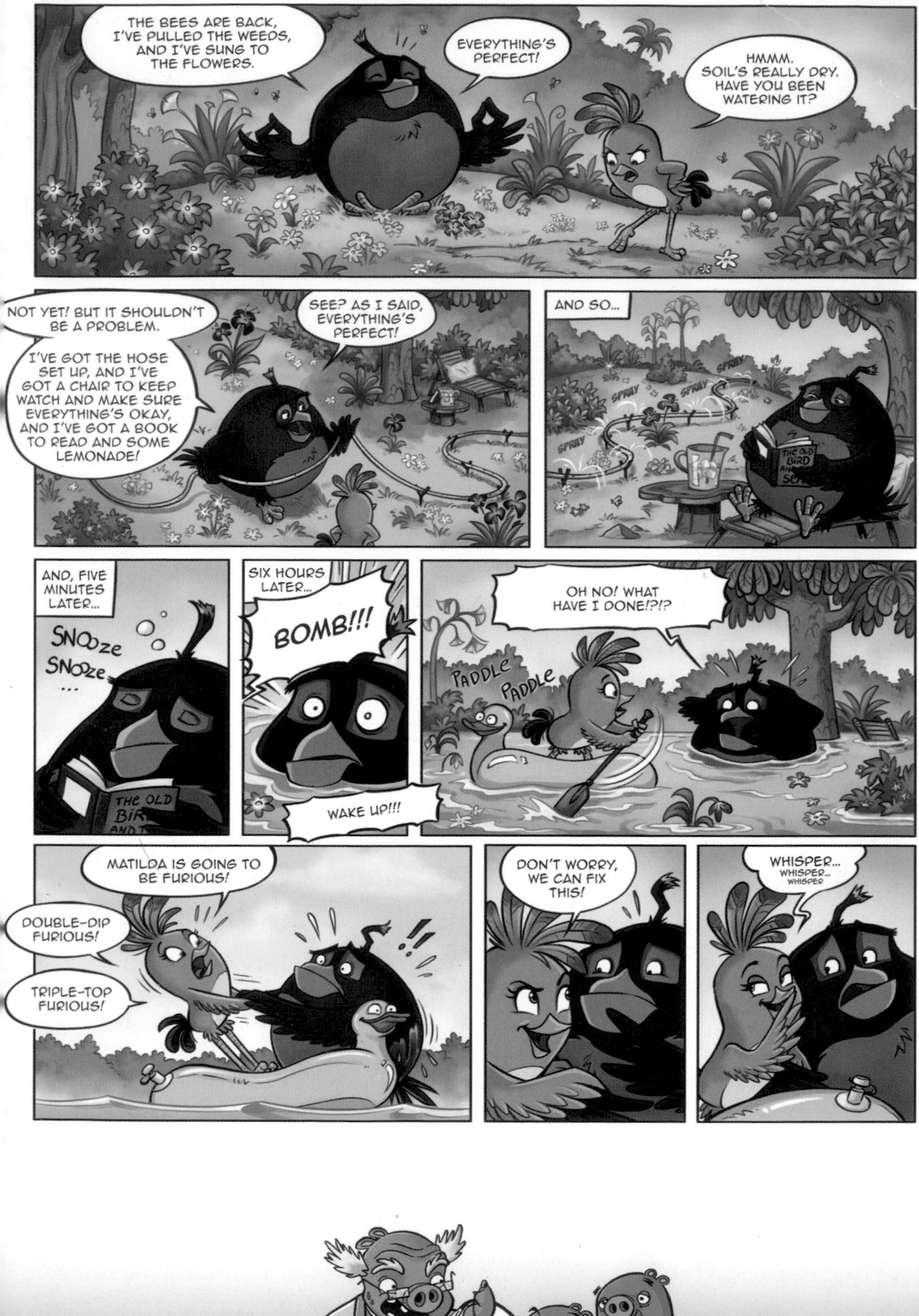
THE BEES ARE BACK, I'VE PULLED THE WEEDS, AND I'VE SUNG TO THE FLOWERS.
EVERYTHING'S PERFECT!
HMMM. SOIL'S REALLY DRY. HAVE YOU BEEN WATERING IT?
NOT YET! BUT IT SHOULDN'T BE A PROBLEM.
I'VE GOT THE HOSE SET UP, AND I'VE GOT A CHAIR TO KEEP WATCH AND MAKE SURE EVERYTHING'S OKAY, AND I'VE GOT A BOOK TO READ AND SOME LEMONADE!
SEE? AS I SAID, EVERYTHING'S PERFECT!
AND SO...
SPRAY
SPRAY
SPRAY
SPRAY
THE OLD BIRD
AND, FIVE MINUTES LATER...
SNOOZE
SNOOZE
...
THE OLD BIR
SIX HOURS LATER...
BOMB!!!
WAKE UP!!!
OH NO! WHAT HAVE I DONE!?!?
PADDLE
PADDLE
MATILDA IS GOING TO BE FURIOUS!
DOUBLE-DIP FURIOUS!
TRIPLE-TOP FURIOUS!
DON'T WORRY, WE CAN FIX THIS!
WHISPER...
WHISPER...
WHISPER

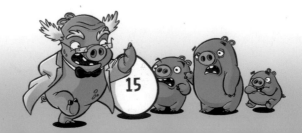

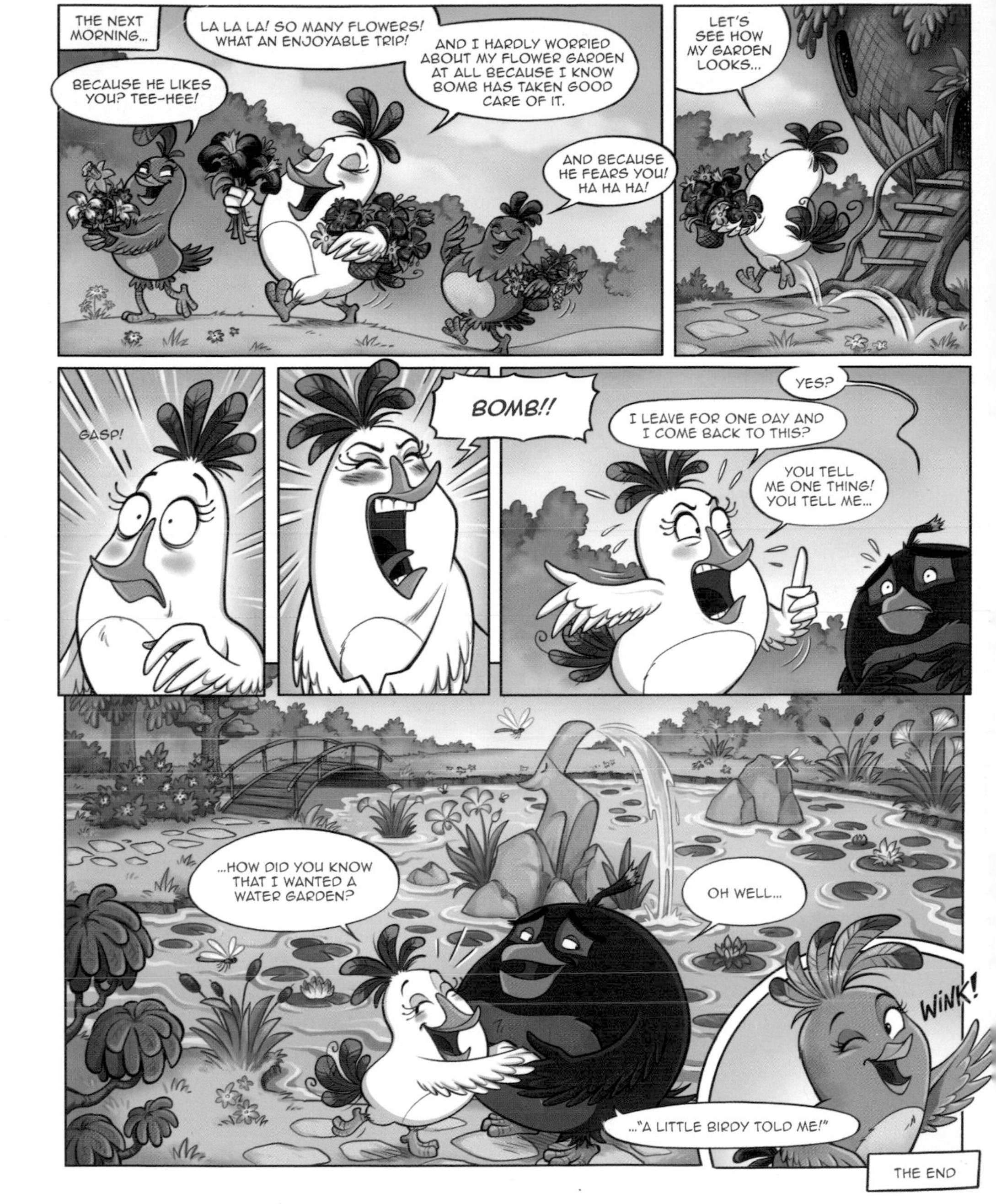
THE NEXT MORNING...
LA LA LA! SO MANY FLOWERS! WHAT AN ENJOYABLE TRIP!
BECAUSE HE LIKES YOU? TEE-HEE!
AND I HARDLY WORRIED ABOUT MY FLOWER GARDEN AT ALL BECAUSE I KNOW BOMB HAS TAKEN GOOD CARE OF IT.
AND BECAUSE HE FEARS YOU! HA HA HA!
LET'S SEE HOW MY GARDEN LOOKS...
GASP!
BOMB!!
YES?
I LEAVE FOR ONE DAY AND I COME BACK TO THIS?
YOU TELL ME ONE THING! YOU TELL ME...
...HOW DID YOU KNOW THAT I WANTED A WATER GARDEN?
OH WELL...
WINK!
..."A LITTLE BIRDY TOLD ME!"
THE END

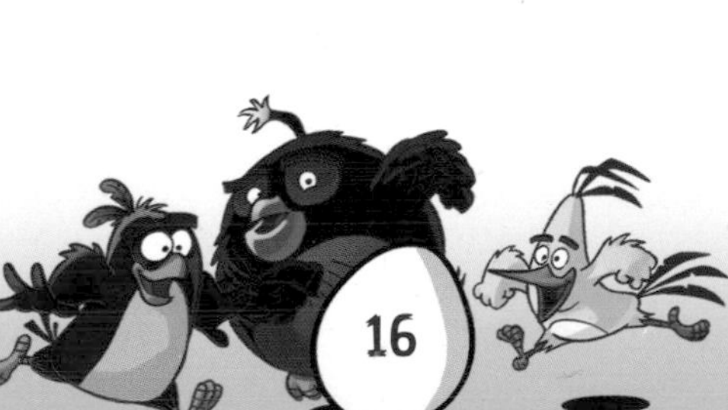

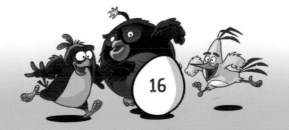

WRITTEN BY: **PAUL TOBIN** • ART BY: **CORRADO MASTANTUONO** • COLORS BY: **NICOLA PASQUETTO** • LETTERS BY: **PISARA OY**

...WE *COURAGEOUSLY* FLY TO BIRD ISLAND!

WE *DRAMATICALLY* LAND ON MIGHTY EAGLE'S MOUNTAINTOP!

WE *HEROICALLY* HAVE LUNCH!

THIS IS A *GOOD* PART OF THE PLAN!

VRRRRRk

THEN WE *FEARLESSLY* CAPTURE MIGHTY EAGLE!

NO MORE! YOU'RE TOO STRONG!

WE *BOLDLY* FLY HIM BACK TO OUR ISLAND!

THEN, A CELEBRATION, BECAUSE WITH MIGHTY EAGLE REMOVED FROM THE PICTURE, OUR NEXT INVASION WILL BE EASY.

HOO-RAH! SNORT! SNORT! HA HA! SNORT!

18

SOON!

THE PLAN IS WORKING! WE'RE INSIDE!

I DON'T THINK WE DID A VERY GOOD JOB OF LUNCH. MAYBE WE SHOULD TRY AGAIN?

THERE HE IS!

ZZZZ! SNORE! SNORK!

ZZZZ! SNORK! SNORE!

CLONK

CLONK CLONK CLONK

CLONK

SNORK! SNORE! ZZZZ!

HMMM. CAN'T EVEN WAKE HIM?

ZZZZ! SNORK! SNORE!

??

ZZZZZZZ! SNORK!

THUMP

OOOF!

CAN I HAVE HIS NEXT LUNCH?

19

MIIIIIIIGHTY EAAAAAAGLE!

MEANWHILE... IN REAL LIFE.

ZZZZZ! SNORK! SNORE!

AHHH!

OOO! MY LUNCHBOX!

PHANTOM PIG PATROL

ZZZZ! SNORK! MIGHTY EAGLE! ZZZZZ! SNORE!

HOLD HIS WINGS! HOLD HIS WINGS!

HERE. I'LL HOLD YOUR LUNCH.

MEANWHILE... IN MIGHTY EAGLE'S DREAMS.

YAY! MIGHTY EAGLE! HE'S SO HANDSOME AND SO REGAL! RAH - RAH RAH! HE'LL THUMP THEM IN THE JAW!

AND... IN REAL LIFE!

RETREAT!

20

ZOOOM

WHEW! SAFE!

LET'S GET OUT OF...

...HERE?

SNORE! ZZZZZ! SNORK!

SMASH

CRASH

SWOOP

ZZZZ! SNORK! SNORE!

PO...

FRRRRRR

AND, IN MIGHTY EAGLE'S DREAMS...

HA HA HA! MIIIIIGHTY EAAAAGLE!

RATTA-TATTA

CLONK

CLONK CLONK

AND, IN REALITY...

SNORE! SNORK! ZZZZZZZZ!

AND SOON...

ZZZZZ! SNORE! ZZZZZ!

ZZZZZZ! SNORE! SNOZZLE- SNORKK !!!

HMM? HOW DID I GET HERE?

I MUST HAVE BEEN SLEEP-WALKING AGAIN.

AND WHAT A *CRAZY* DREAM!

THOSE PIGS ATTACKING *HERE*?

THAT WOULD *NEVER* HAPPEN.

ZZZZ! SNORK! SNORE!

THE END

22

ANGRY BIRDS

No Bird is an Island

LIFE IN THE BIRD VILLAGE TAKES SOME GETTING USED TO...

AND HE *SCOOORES!*

UNGH!

TUM

TOK

SPUT

A TOUGH MATCH! WANNA JOIN?

NO, I'VE GOT A HEADACHE.

I LOVE THESE BOYS, BUT THEY *DO* MAKE A LOT OF NOISE!

GLUGLUGLU

WRITTEN BY: **KARI KORHONEN** • ART BY: **MARCO GERVASIO** • INKS BY: **ALESSANDRO ZEMOLIN**
COLORS BY: **NICOLA PASQUETTO** • LETTERS BY: **PISARA OY**

23

NOT TO MENTION THE VILLAGE OUTSIDE!

EARLY BIRD WORMS

LATE RISER WORMS

NO WORMS TODAY

I'M NOT USED TO THE CONSTANT CHIRPING, THE ENDLESS HUSTLE AND BUSTLE!

EARLY BIRD WORMS

IT'S A FAR CRY FROM MY OLD ABODE AT THE BEACH!

"THERE, MY ONLY COMPANY WAS THE SOUND OF THE SEA LAPPING AGAINST THE SHORE!"

SOMETIMES A BIT OF PEACE AND QUIET WOULD BE...

GOAL!

24

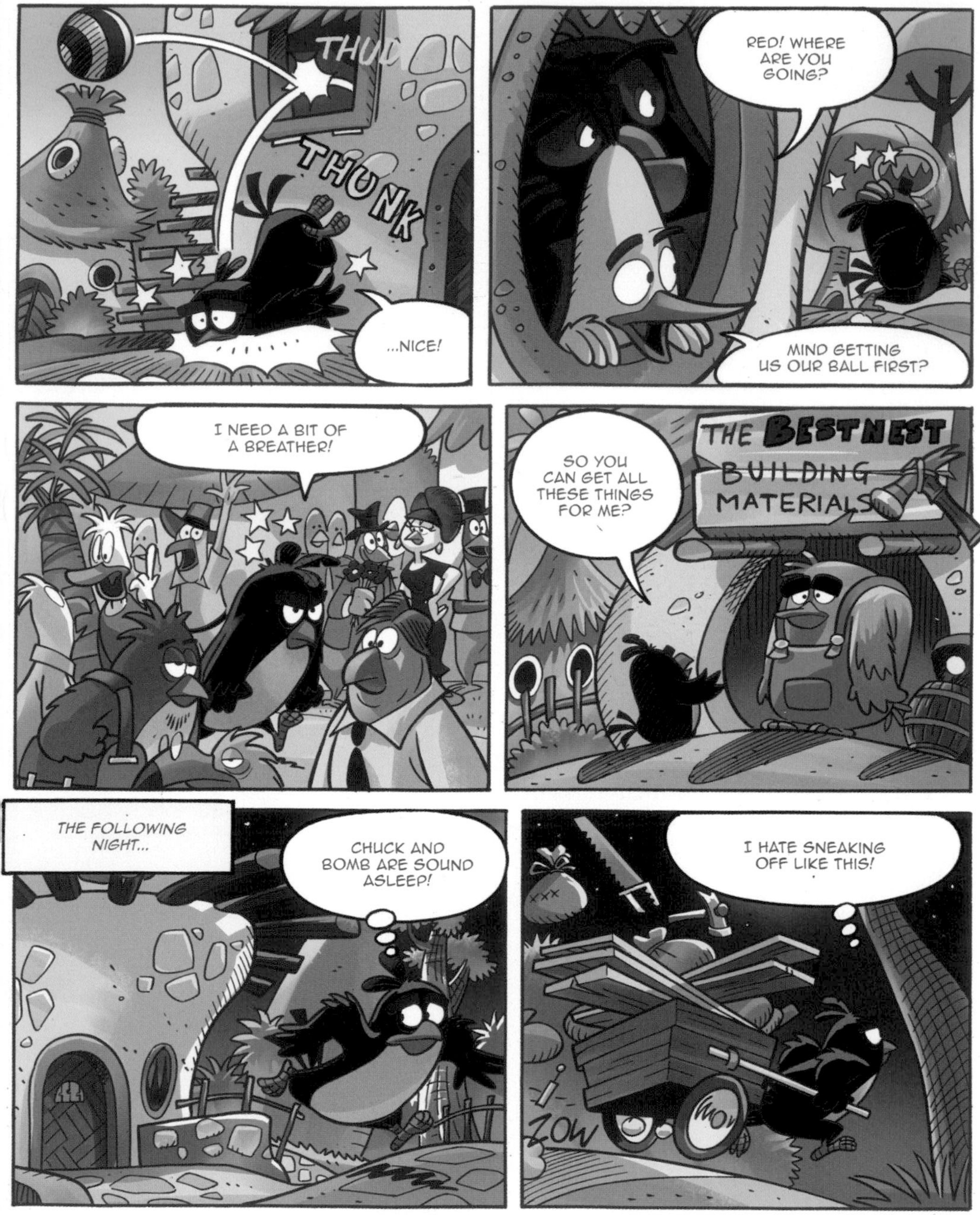
THUD
THUNK
...NICE!
RED! WHERE ARE YOU GOING?
MIND GETTING US OUR BALL FIRST?
I NEED A BIT OF A BREATHER!
THE BESTNEST BUILDING MATERIALS
SO YOU CAN GET ALL THESE THINGS FOR ME?
THE FOLLOWING NIGHT...
CHUCK AND BOMB ARE SOUND ASLEEP!
I HATE SNEAKING OFF LIKE THIS!
ZOW

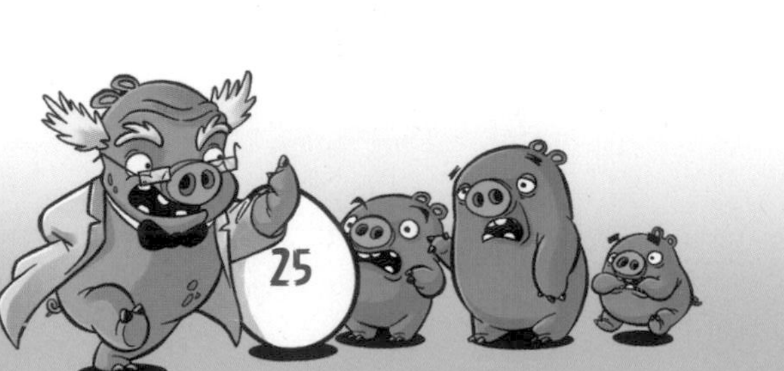

EVERYONE'S TRIED TO MAKE ME FEEL VERY WELCOME!

I CAN'T VERY WELL SAY: "THANKS' BUT I'M OFF!" I DON'T WANT TO *HURT* ANYONE'S *FEELINGS!*

ISN'T THAT THAT RED BIRD?

THE FAMOUS ONE?

WHERE'S HE OFF TO AT THIS HOUR?

SOON, IN A DISTANT CORNER OF BIRD ISLAND CALLED SILENT COVE...

KNOCK KNOCK
BANG BANG

26

PERFECT, IF I DO SAY SO MYSELF!

WHEN CITY LIFE GETS TO BE A BIT MUCH...

PLONF

...I CAN ALWAYS COME HERE FOR A BIT OF *REST AND RELAXATION!*

NO ONE HAS TO KNOW ABOUT MY LITTLE HIDEAWAY! MY *COUNTRY COTTAGE!*

27

MY LITTLE PIECE OF PARADISE!

A FEW DAYS LATER...

LOOK! RED'S OFF AGAIN!

HE SAYS HE TAKES *LONG WALKS!* WHO WALKS RATHER THAN PLAYS BALL?

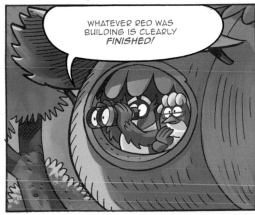

WHATEVER RED WAS BUILDING IS CLEARLY *FINISHED!*

IT MUST BE A *RETREAT* OF SOME SORT!

A COTTAGE IN THE JUNGLE?

INDEED!

SIGH!

IT SURE IS QUIET HERE.

ALMOST *TOO* QUIET.

NOT A SINGLE CHIRP. NOT EVEN A SQUAWK.

HONESTLY! IS THIS NORMAL?

SPLONF

I'M SO *BORED* I COULD CRY!

FINALLY! SIGNS OF LIFE!

CLONK BANG BANG

MORE CABIN BUILDERS?

BANG BANG BANG

LOVE THE QUIET! LEAVING BIRD VILLAGE WAS A *WONDERFUL IDEA!*

WE ARE VERY QUIET BIRDS! THE FORCED FLOCKING WAS DRIVING US CUCKOO!

THE ENDLESS, INANE CHIRPING! I CAN'T SLEEP!

THE FEATHERS THAT FLY IN HEAVY TRAFFIC! AWFUL!

DON'T WORRY, YOU WON'T EVEN KNOW WE ARE HERE!

SILENT COVE IS THE MOST BEAUTIFUL SPOT ON THE ISLAND!

ACTUALLY, I DON'T MIND THE COMPANY!

I CAN EVEN HELP YOU BUILD YOUR CABIN, IF YOU LIKE!

BOM BANG BAM

WHEN THE WORD SPREADS, EVEN MORE BIRDS SEEKING SOLITUDE ARRIVE...

SUCH SWEET PEACE!

THE QUIET OF THE COUNTRYSIDE!

I HAVE *YEARS* OF EXPERIENCE IN THE *QUIET LIFE!*

I'M HAPPY TO SPREAD THAT MESSAGE LOUDLY!

TOGETHER WE WORK TWICE AS FAST, EH?

NOW, WHAT I WOULD DO HERE, IS....

DOESN'T HE EVER *LEAVE?*

31

SOON RED'S NEED FOR COMPANY RUFFLES FEATHERS...

HI-DE-HO, NEIGHBOR!

JUST HERE TO CHECK YOUR BUILD!

SOON, IN SILENT COVE...

SHUT YOUR BEAKS! I'M CALLING THIS MEETING TO ORDER!

RED JUST *DROPS IN* UN-ANNOUNCED!

HE BEGINS SENTENCES WITH *"IF I MAY OFFER A SUGGESTION..."*

AND *"WHAT I WOULD DO HERE..."*!

HE THINKS THAT HIS YEARS ON THE BEACH MADE HIM THE *KING OF CABINS!*

WE ALL CAME HERE TO GET AWAY FROM IT ALL!

THE ENDLESS CHATTER!

THE UNSOLICITED ADVICE!

32

CLEARLY SOMETHING MUST BE DO--

THUD

UHH!

HA-HA-HA! YOU GO AND GET IT!

WHAT *IS* THAT RACKET?!

YOU'LL GET IT LATER! YOU BROUGHT PLENTY OF BALLS!

I'M SO GLAD YOU CAME OVER, GUYS!

THIS PLACE JUST WASN'T THE SAME WITHOUT YOU!

WHAT'S UP WITH YOU, THUNDERBIRDS?

BANISHED FROM MY OWN HOLIDAY COMMUNITY!

THE PLACE I HELPED SET UP! THE NERVE OF SOME BIRDS!

YOU'D GROWN TIRED OF THE QUIET ANYWAY, RIGHT?

NOT THAT THIS PLACE IS SUCH A HEAVING METROPOLIS RIGHT NOW!

EARLY BIRD WORMS

LATE RISER WORMS

NO WORM TODAY

CLOSED AGAIN

EVERYBODY MIGRATED TO THE COUNTRY! THEY GOT THE *CABIN FEVER* FROM YOU!

DON'T WORRY, THE TOWN WON'T STAY QUIET FOR LONG!

WITH YOU TWO AROUND? I BELIEVE YA!

THE END

ANGRY BIRDS
SWIFT JUSTICE

GOOD MORNING, JUDGE!

READY TO BALANCE THE SCALES OF JUSTICE?

ABM 2016-009

MERE *WHINERS* AND *MALCONTENTS* LOOKING FOR *ME* TO SETTLE THEIR PETTY FEUDS!

DON'T TALK TO ME ABOUT JUSTICE, CYRUS! I'M *FED UP* WITH JUSTICE!

WRITTEN BY: KARI KORHONEN • ART BY: GIORGIO CAVAZZANO • INKS BY: ALESSANDRO ZEMOLIN
COLORS BY: DIGIKORE • LETTERS BY: PISARA OY

35

OH, SWELL! ANOTHER FULL DOCKET!

JUST LOOK AT THESE DESPERATE SOULS!

I WAS ORDERED HERE BECAUSE OF MY *SPEEDING TICKETS!*

AND MINE IS THE *36TH* CASE IN LINE!

I CAN'T BE HERE ALL DAY!

WOOSH!

I'VE GOT PLACES TO GO! BIRDS TO MEET!

LET'S SEE IF WE CAN'T *SPEED THINGS UP* A BIT!

...AND HE REFUSES TO GIVE ME A REFUND!

JUST LOOK AT THESE BERRIES HE SOLD ME! THERE ARE *HARDLY ANY WORMS* IN THEM!

THERE'S *NOUT* WRONG WITH MY BERRIES!

NOT ENOUGH WORMS!

WHEN PEOPLE ASK ME: "WHY DO YOU GET UP IN THE MORNING, JUDGE?", THIS...

WOOSH!

I CAN HELP!

37

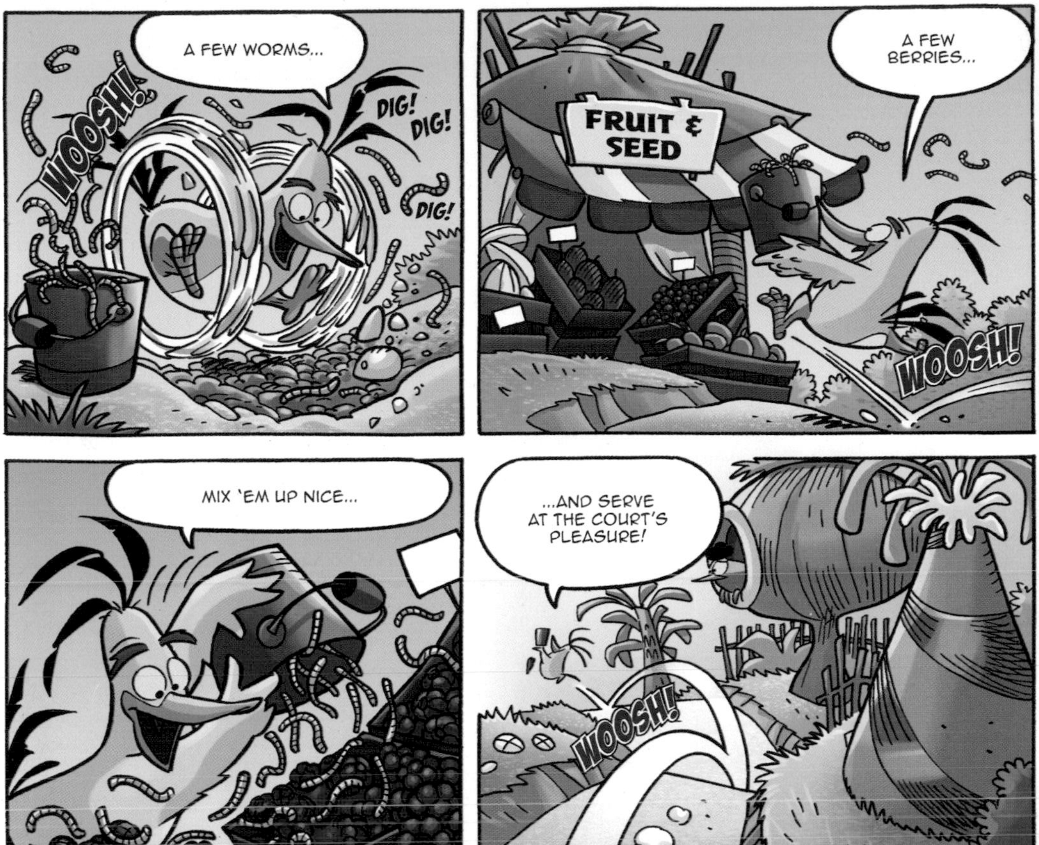
A FEW WORMS...
WOOSH!
DIG!
DIG!
DIG!
FRUIT & SEED
A FEW BERRIES...
WOOSH!
MIX 'EM UP NICE...
...AND SERVE AT THE COURT'S PLEASURE!
WOOSH!
...IS *JUST* THE SORT OF CASE I GIVE THEM AS A REPLY!
A POINT OF ORDER, YOUR HONOR!
I BOUGHT THESE BERRIES THIS MORNING, YOUR HONOR! LOOK!

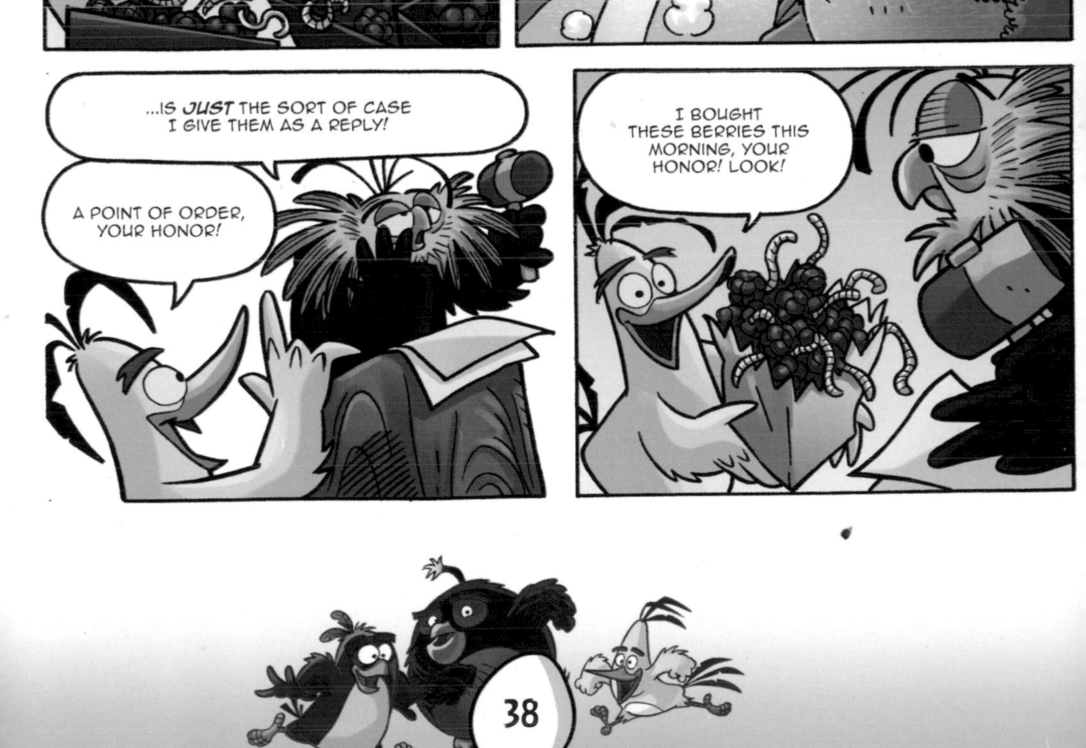

THEY ARE POSITIVELY *ALIVE* WITH MAGGOTS AND WORMS!

THESE REALLY *ARE* JUST AS THEY SHOULD BE!

SEE? A PERFECT MAGGOT-TO-BERRY RATIO!

IT WAS MY *REPUTATION* I WAS WORRIED ABOUT! I'LL GLADLY REPLACE YOUR BERRIES!

DISMISSED! NEXT CASE!

KNOCK!

MY NEIGHBOR'S *TUBA PLAYING* IS DRIVING ME NUTS, YOUR LORDSHIP!

I'M TEETERING ON THE BRINK OF A NERVOUS C-C-COLLAPSE, YOUR HIGHNESS!

AND WHAT SAY THE DEFENDANT?

I *LOOOVES* MY TUBA!

THAT'S NICE AND CLEAR, THANK YOU. THE COURT FEELS IT MUST *INSPECT* THE SITE...

LET'S SPEED THINGS UP AGAIN...

WOOSH!

KLONK!

KLONK!

KLONK!

...WITH A *BIT OF BUILDING!*

...BEFORE IT CAN RENDER A VERDICT!

T-THAT WASN'T THERE BEFORE!

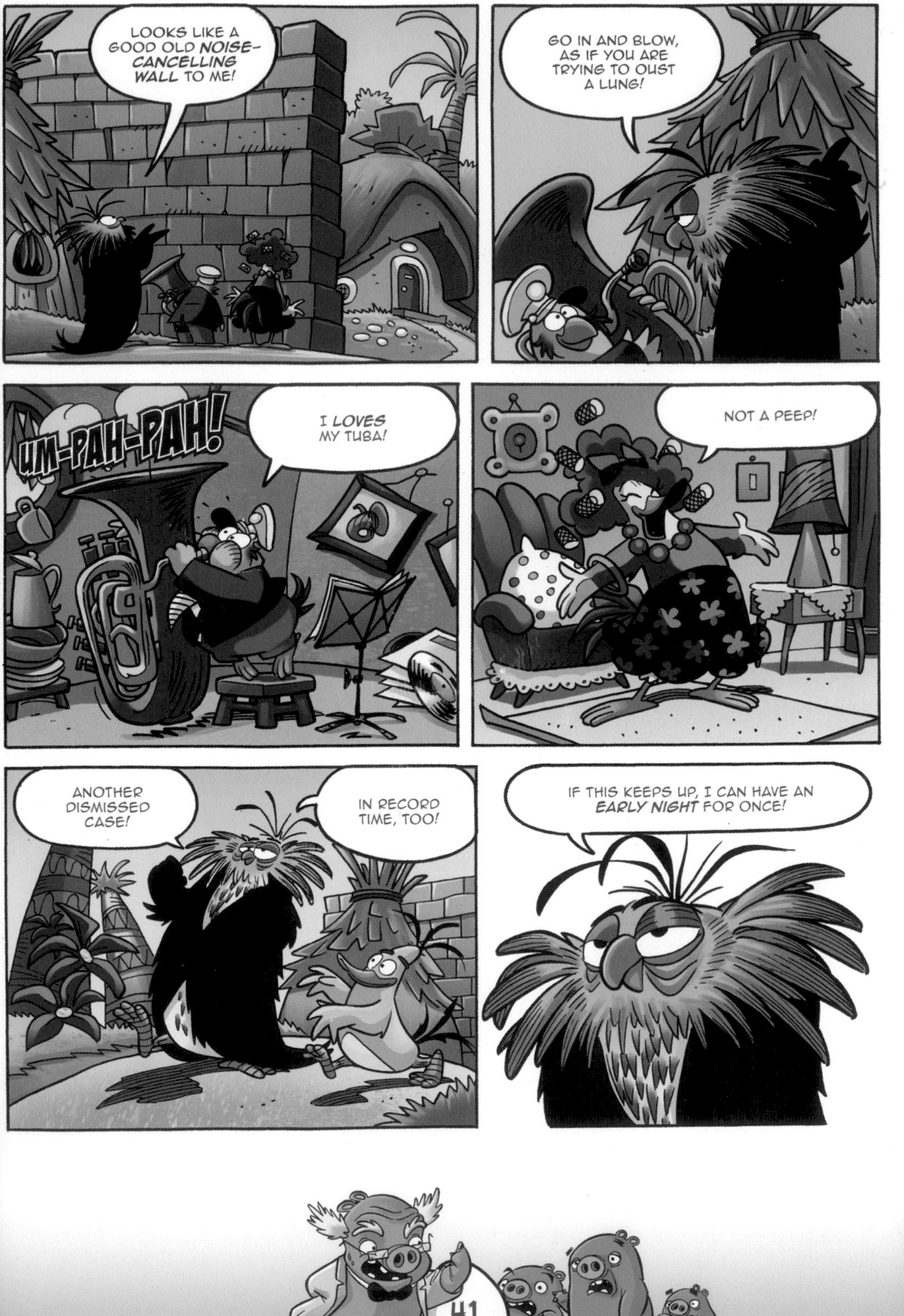
LOOKS LIKE A GOOD OLD NOISE-CANCELLING WALL TO ME!
GO IN AND BLOW, AS IF YOU ARE TRYING TO OUST A LUNG!
UM-PAH-PAH!
I LOVES MY TUBA!
NOT A PEEP!
ANOTHER DISMISSED CASE!
IN RECORD TIME, TOO!
IF THIS KEEPS UP, I CAN HAVE AN EARLY NIGHT FOR ONCE!

IT DOES KEEP UP!

THE CHARGES AGAINST YOU ARE HEAVY, MONSIER STEALITALLANDHOW!

ON TOP OF EVERYTHING, THE COURT SUSPECTS YOU HAVE GIVEN A FALSE NAME! THIS WILL TAKE *FOREVER!*

SIR!

ON THE BASIS OF THIS *NEW TESTIMONY*, NOT AT ALL HASTILY GATHERED, I DECLARE YOU *INNOCENT!*

YOU ARE FREE TO GO, MONSIER STEALITALLANDHOW! SOON, SO SHALL *I!*

AND SO...

CASE #36!

FINALLY!

SIR! HELP!

WE NEED YOUR HELP!

42

THESE FRAUDSTERS CLAIM THEY GOT *SICK* EATING MY BERRIES!

THE WORMS... WERE *INEDIBLE!* BURP!

THERE'S *NOUT* WRONG WITH MY BERRIES!

YOUR MAJESTY! *THE WALL!*

IT WAS HASTILY BUILT AND *COLLAPSED* ON OUR NEIGHBORS!

WE WAS IN-JURED!

I JUST *LOOOVES* MY TUBA!

WE WANT TO *SUE!*

SUE!

SUE!

MONSIER STEAL... WHATSIT WENT ON A *CRIME SPREE.* NOT SURPRISING, REALLY.

43

TILT!

PUT US ON THE DOCKET *NOW!*

THUD

OH DEAR!

NOW WHAT DO WE DO...

COSTUMES & FEATHERS

I NEED TO FIX THIS!

WOOSH!

...FOR *JUSTICE* IN BIRD VILLAGE?

THIS IS THE WORST IDEA *EVER!*

IF THESE CRAZIES ARE STILL ON THE LIST TOMORROW, THE JUDGE MAY *NEVER* RECOVER!

THE COURT WILL COME TO ORDER!

YOU'D THINK THAT CHAOS WOULD ENSUE, WOULDN'T YOU?

ACCORDING TO THIS STATUTE HERE...

...I FIND FOR THE *PLAINTIFF!*

BIRD LAW

IT'S IN *TAWNY FROGMOUTH VS. HOARY PUFFLEG!* YOU'RE DOING *GREAT!*

WHEW! WHO KNEW JUDGING WAS SUCH *HARD WORK!*

COME EVENING...

THE DOCKET HAS BEEN *CLEARED?*

IT'S A *MIRACLE!*

I'LL RIP UP YOUR SPEEDING TICKETS, DEAR BOY!
YOU MUST PROMISE NEVER TO TELL WHAT HAPPENED HERE TODAY!
BUT SOON...
STOP RIGHT THERE, CHUCK!
!
I'VE HAD RELIABLE REPORTS YOU'VE BEEN SPEEDING ALL OVER TOWN TODAY!
IF YOU WANT TO CONTEST THIS TICKET, FEEL FREE TO TAKE IT UP WITH THE COURT!
TILT!
THE END.

ZEN WITH A SLICE OF HAM

ABM 2016-007

ANGRY BIRDS

HIGH ABOVE THE OCEAN, NEAR BIRD ISLAND...

PUT

MAYDAY! MAYDAY! PORK OGH CALLING PIGGY TOWER, OVER!

SPUT

PUT

PUT

I'M GOING IN HARD, OVER!

PUT POT

PET

POT

MY TRIP IS WELL AND TRULY OVER, OVER!

①

WRITTEN BY: **KARI KORHONEN** • ART BY: **THOMAS CABELLIC** • COLORS BY: **DIGIKORE** • LETTERS BY: **PISARA OY**

47

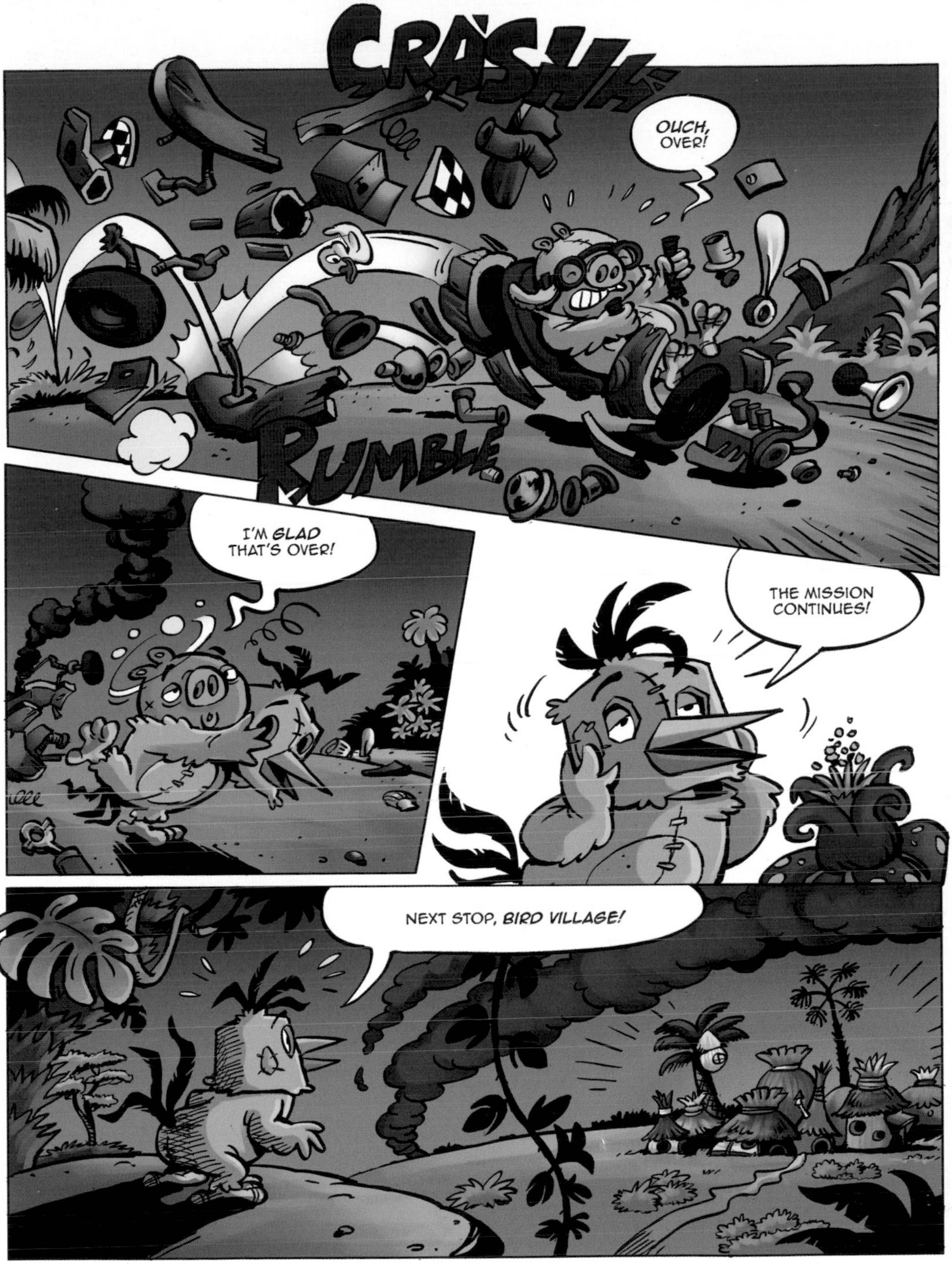
CRASH!
OUCH, OVER!
RUMBLE
I'M GLAD THAT'S OVER!
THE MISSION CONTINUES!
NEXT STOP, BIRD VILLAGE!

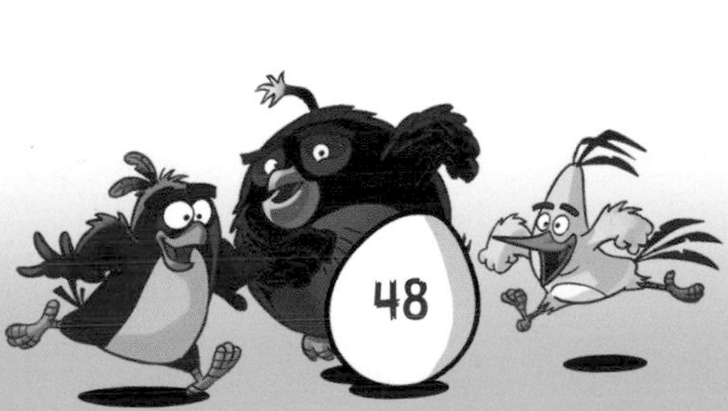

MORNING.

YOU LOOK PLEASED, MATILDA!

MATILDA'S WELLFARE CENTER

BIRD COURT IS SENDING US *A NEW PUPIL* FOR OUR ANGER MANAGEMENT CLASS! HIS NAME IS *CEDRIC!*

CEDRIC HAS A PROBLEM WITH *SWEARING!* JUDGE THINKS I CAN CURE HIM!

IS THAT THE DUDE?

YOO HOO! THERE'S NOTHING TO BE SCARED OF!

COME JOIN US!

GULP! DISCOVERED ALREADY?

③

DON'T RUN! EVERYBODY RUNS! I ALWAYS CATCH THEM!

THIS IS FOR YOUR OWN GOOD, CEDRIC!

MORNING'S GROUP THERAPY BEGINS...

WHO WOULD LIKE TO SHARE FIRST? CEDRIC? RED?

MY MISSION WAS TO SPY AND *FIND WEAKNESSES* IN THE BIRD ISLAND DEFENSE!

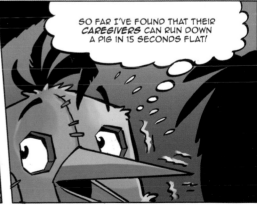

SO FAR I'VE FOUND THAT THEIR *CAREGIVERS* CAN RUN DOWN A PIG IN 15 SECONDS FLAT!

AND THE *BIG, SCARY ONES* ARE CLEARLY OFF THEIR ROCKER!

GRUNT!

CHUCK! SHOW THE NEW GUY HOW IT'S DONE!

...AND THEN THE FELLA SAID I WAS RUNNING TOO FAST AND THAT I WASN'T SUPPOSED TODOTHATBUTWHOISHETOTELLMEWHAT- TODOANDWHEREDOESHEGETOFF...

...IFELTSOMUCHLIKEPUNCHINGHIMBUT- THENHEWASALLLIKE"CALLTHEPOLICE!"AND- STUFFANDIWASLIKEI'MOUTTAHEREANDWHY- SHOULDITAKETHISBUTIWELLANDTRULY- WENTHOMEANDTRASHEDACOUPLEOF- PILLOWSCAUSEIWASSOMAD... SO MAD!

BLINK!

BLINK!

SOMEBODY ELSE? *ANYBODY ELSE?*

YUP! POSITIVELY *CERTIFIABLE!*

51

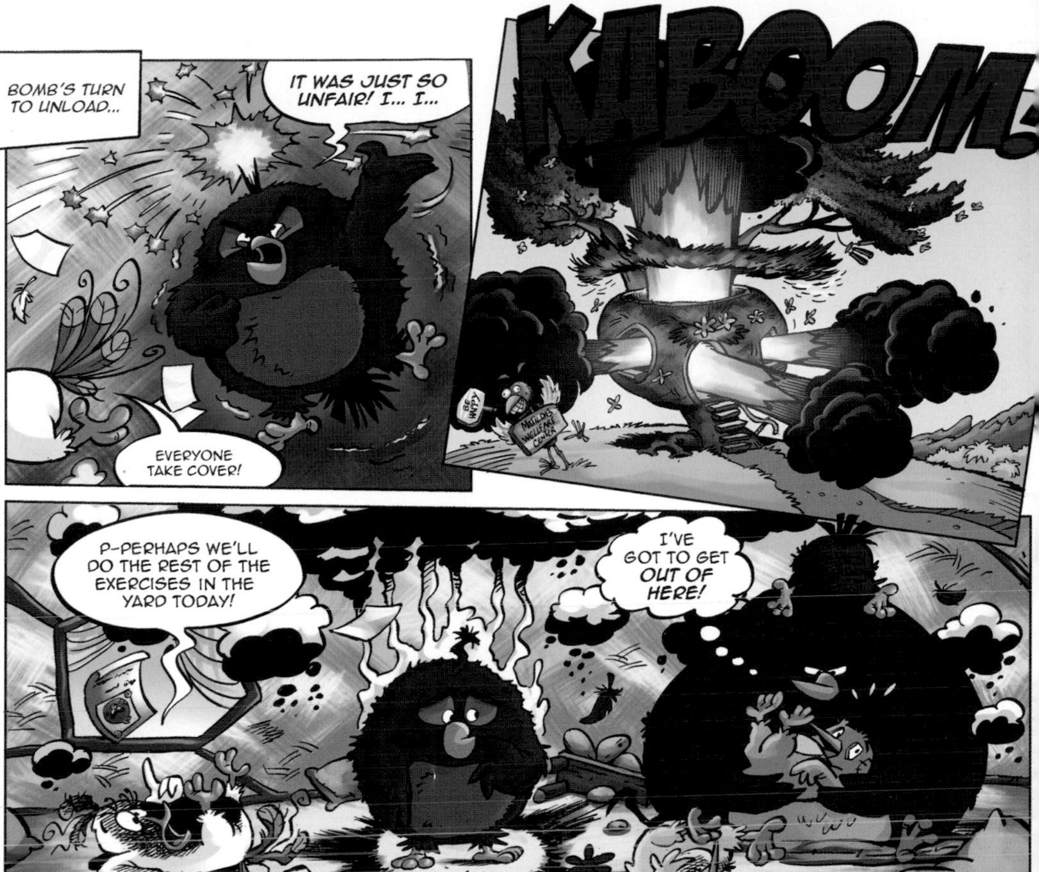
BOMB'S TURN TO UNLOAD...
IT WAS JUST SO UNFAIR! I... I...
EVERYONE TAKE COVER!
KABOOM
P-PERHAPS WE'LL DO THE REST OF THE EXERCISES IN THE YARD TODAY!
I'VE GOT TO GET OUT OF HERE!
THE TEACHER KEEPS WATCHING ME LIKE A HAWK!
MY BEST BET IS TO LEARN THIS STUFF QUICKLY AND HOPE SHE LOSES INTEREST!
A PERFECT "BALANCING BABOON", CEDRIC! YOU'RE A NATURAL!
6

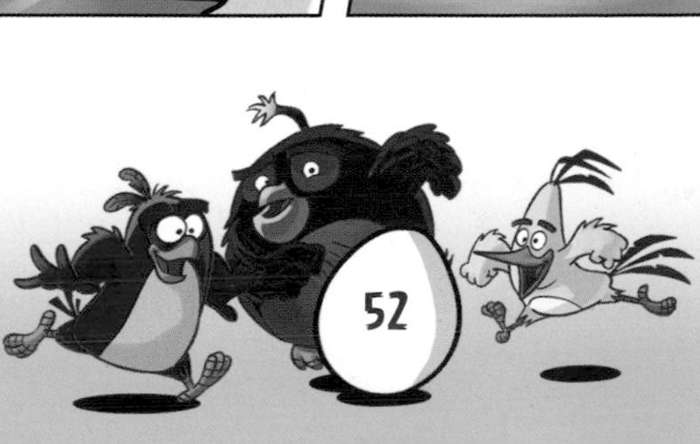

WHILE SHE'S NOT LOOKING...

NOT LIKE THAT, TERENCE!

YOU ARE MY *STAR PUPIL* NOW! COME AND SHOW TERENCE HOW IT'S DONE!

A FEW DAYS LATER...

STRENGTH THROUGH INNER PEACE... OMMMM...

SUCH *CALM!* SUCH *GRACE!*

I HAVE *NEVER* BEEN THIS PROUD, MY LITTLE *PRODIGY!*

PROUD ENOUGH TO BOAST!

HE USED TO CURSE LIKE A SAILOR, BUT *NOW* LOOK AT HIM!

WHAT A *NICE YOUNG MAN!*

YOU REALLY ARE THE BEST, MATILDA!

"NICE YOUNG MAN?" EVERYONE IS SO *KIND* HERE! AND THE VILLAGE IS *SO BEAUTIFUL!*

"BACK ON PIGGY ISLAND I'M A LOWLY WORKER WHO GETS SHOUTED AT 24/7!"

HERE, I AM A NICE GUY AND A *PRODIGY!* I'M SO HAPPY I COULD CRY!

THERE'S SOMETHING *FISHY* ABOUT THIS CEDRIC CHARACTER!

HE HAS A *CURSING PROBLEM*, BUT I HAVEN'T EVEN HEARD A FOUL SYLLABLE!

⑧

MATILDA HAS SUCH A GRIP ON HIM, I HAVEN'T BEEN ABLE TO FIND OUT MORE!

GLUE

54

BUT EVENTUALLY...

ADMIRING THE VIEW, CEDRIC?

!

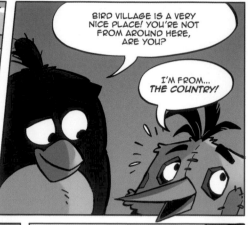

BIRD VILLAGE IS A VERY NICE PLACE! YOU'RE NOT FROM AROUND HERE, ARE YOU?

I'M FROM... THE COUNTRY!

BIRD VILLAGE IS THE BEST PLACE I'VE EVER SEEN!

I WOULD DEARLY LIKE TO STAY, BUT I'M NOT SURE I CAN!

SURE YOU CAN! WE JUST NEED TO FIND SOMETHING YOU'RE GOOD AT FOR YOU TO DO! I HAVE A SUGGESTION...

AND SO...

LADIES! WELCOME! READY FOR "ZEN OF PECKING" FOR BEGINNERS?

MATILDA'S WELLFARE CENTER

HAPPY

SMILE

SORRY, MATILDA!
WE ARE GOING TO CLASSES ELSEWHERE NOW!
?
WHAT?!?
STEP RIGHT IN! I'M SURE WE CAN FIT EVERYONE!
WE'LL START WITH SOME LIGHT MEDITATION TO GET IN TOUCH WITH OUR INNER CHAKRA...
GURU CEDRIC IS SIMPLY THE BEST!
STEP AWAY FROM THE ANGER! REMEMBER YOUR BREATHING EXERCISES!

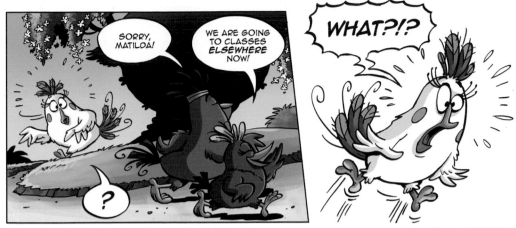

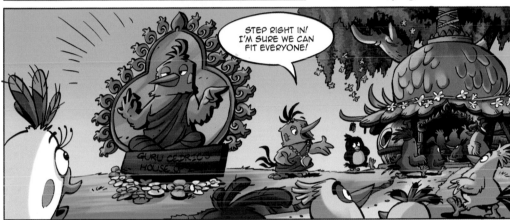

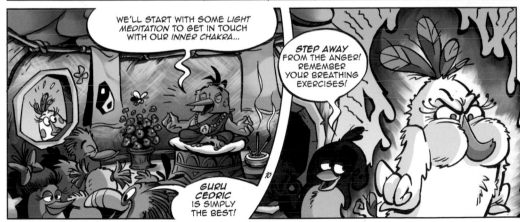

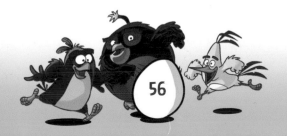

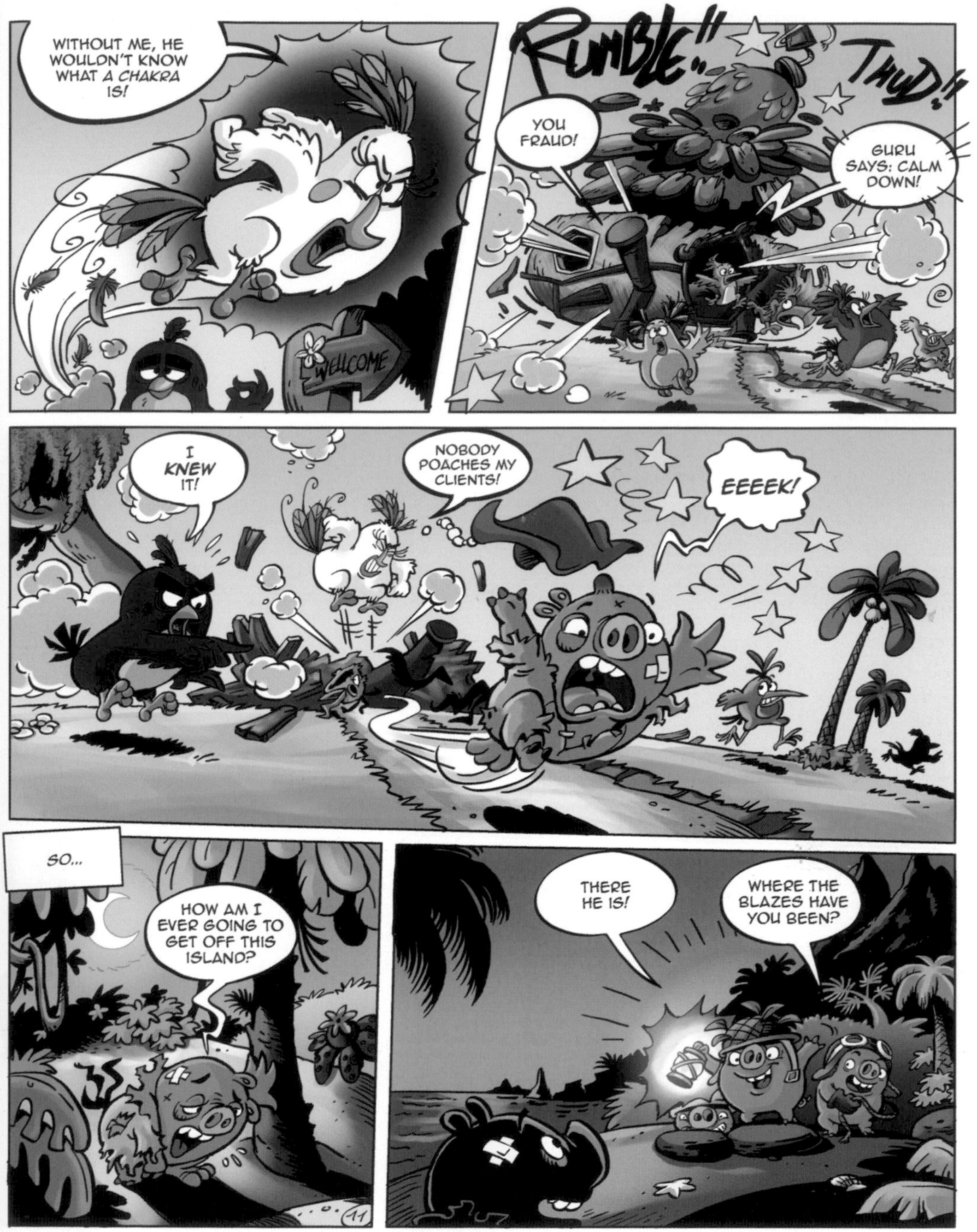
WITHOUT ME, HE WOULDN'T KNOW WHAT A CHAKRA IS!
WELLCOME
RUMBLE!!
THUD!!
YOU FRAUD!
GURU SAYS: CALM DOWN!
I KNEW IT!
NOBODY POACHES MY CLIENTS!
EEEEK!
SO...
HOW AM I EVER GOING TO GET OFF THIS ISLAND?
THERE HE IS!
WHERE THE BLAZES HAVE YOU BEEN?

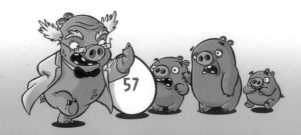

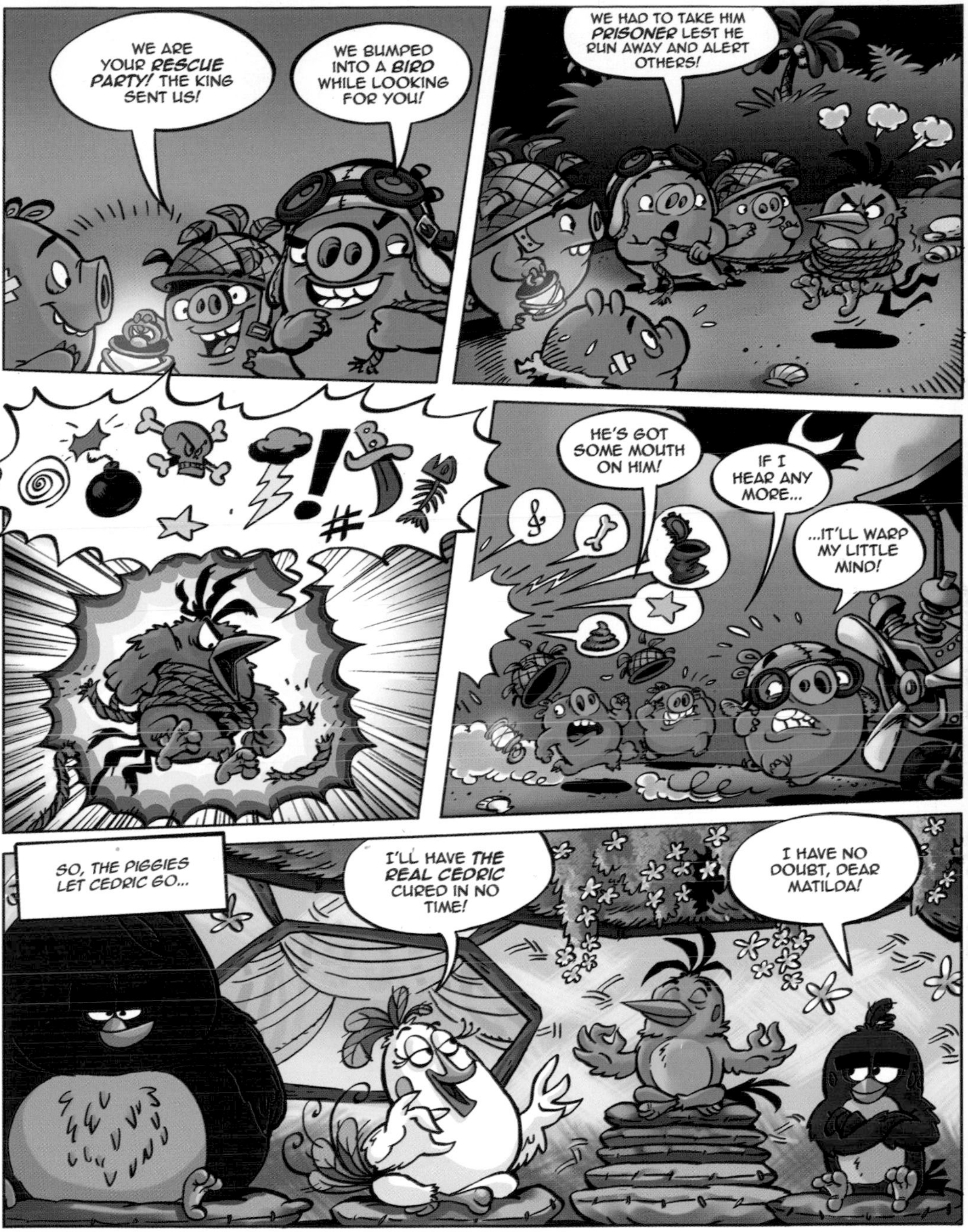
WE ARE YOUR RESCUE PARTY! THE KING SENT US!
WE BUMPED INTO A BIRD WHILE LOOKING FOR YOU!
WE HAD TO TAKE HIM PRISONER LEST HE RUN AWAY AND ALERT OTHERS!
HE'S GOT SOME MOUTH ON HIM!
IF I HEAR ANY MORE...
...IT'LL WARP MY LITTLE MIND!
SO, THE PIGGIES LET CEDRIC GO...
I'LL HAVE THE REAL CEDRIC CURED IN NO TIME!
I HAVE NO DOUBT, DEAR MATILDA!

Written by: **Paul Tobin** • Art by: **Cesar Ferioli** • Colors by: **Digikore** • Letters by: **Pisara Oy**

UNFORTUNATELY, OUR ROYAL LARDERS ARE ENTIRELY DEVOID OF THIS RARE MUSHROOM, SO YOU THREE PIGS MUST SEARCH IN THE *ONLY* PLACE WHERE THE MUSHROOMS ARE KNOWN TO GROW.

CERTAIN DOOM CAVERNS.

AHH?

OH!

CAN'T WE JUST GO TO CERTAIN FUN AMUSEMENT PARK?

NO NO NO.

ALL THAT YOU'D FIND THERE ARE...

"...TUMMY TUM TUM TAFFIES AND...

"...DEEP FRIED PUMPKIN PIES, AND THE NUMBER ONE AMUSEMENT PARK RIDE...

"...THE UNMOVING COUCH."

BUT WHAT YOU *WON'T* FIND IS A *PORKINI MUSHROOM*, SO IT'S OFF TO CERTAIN DOOM CAVERNS FOR YOU.

THUMP

THUMP

THUMP

60

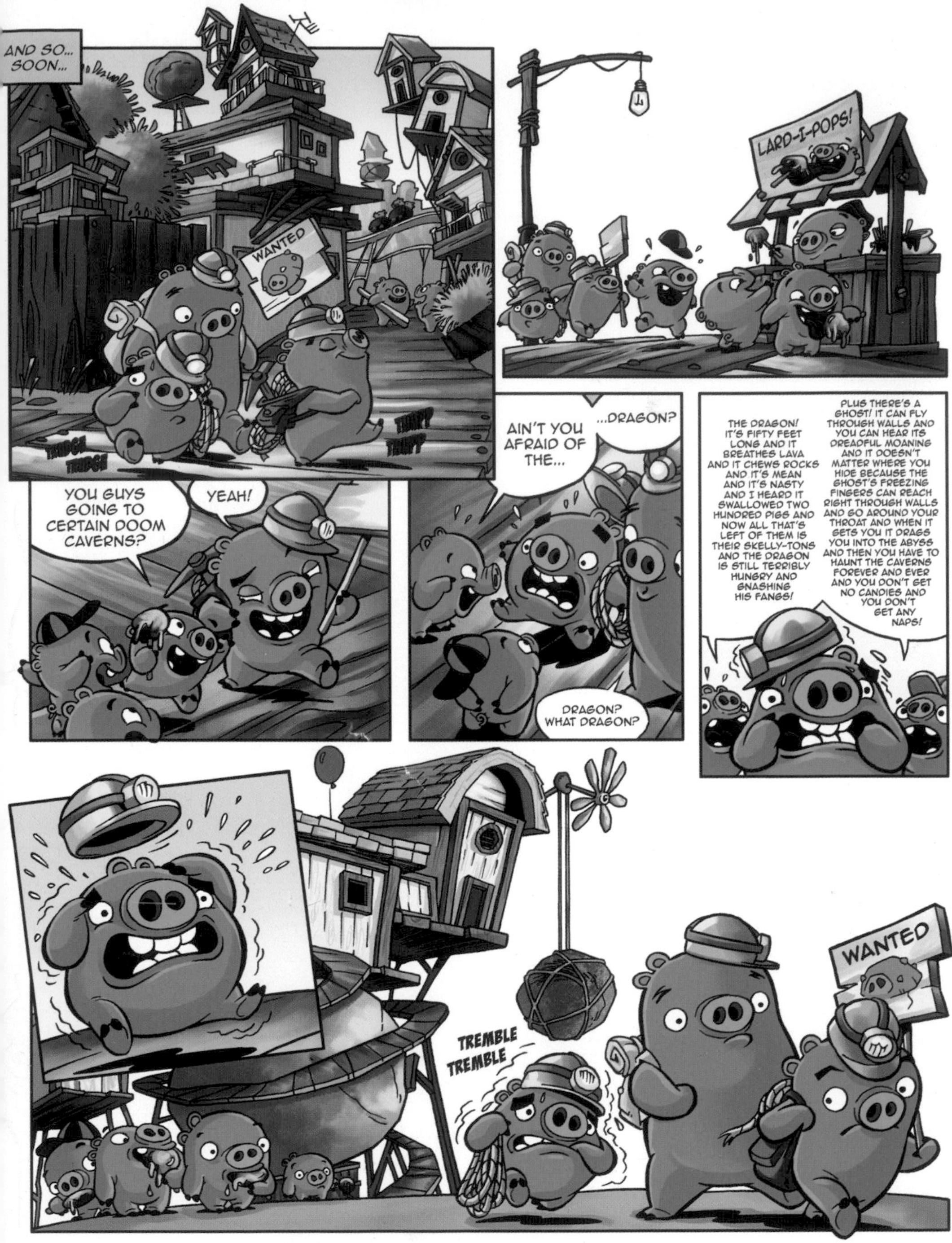
AND SO... SOON...
WANTED
TRUDGE TRUDGE
LARD-I-POPS!
YOU GUYS GOING TO CERTAIN DOOM CAVERNS?
YEAH!
AIN'T YOU AFRAID OF THE...
...DRAGON?
DRAGON? WHAT DRAGON?
THE DRAGON! IT'S FIFTY FEET LONG AND IT BREATHES LAVA AND IT CHEWS ROCKS AND IT'S MEAN AND IT'S NASTY AND I HEARD IT SWALLOWED TWO HUNDRED PIGS AND NOW ALL THAT'S LEFT OF THEM IS THEIR SKELLY-TONS AND THE DRAGON IS STILL TERRIBLY HUNGRY AND GNASHING HIS FANGS!
PLUS THERE'S A GHOST! IT CAN FLY THROUGH WALLS AND YOU CAN HEAR ITS DREADFUL MOANING AND IT DOESN'T MATTER WHERE YOU HIDE BECAUSE THE GHOST'S FREEZING FINGERS CAN REACH RIGHT THROUGH WALLS AND GO AROUND YOUR THROAT AND WHEN IT GETS YOU IT DRAGS YOU INTO THE ABYSS AND THEN YOU HAVE TO HAUNT THE CAVERNS FOREVER AND EVER AND YOU DON'T GET NO CANDIES AND YOU DON'T GET ANY NAPS!
TREMBLE TREMBLE
WANTED

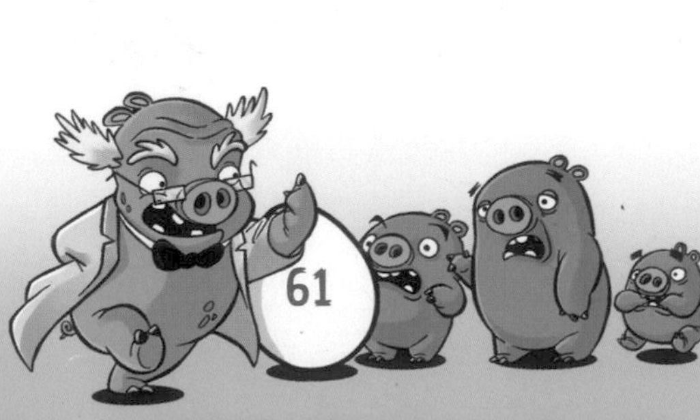

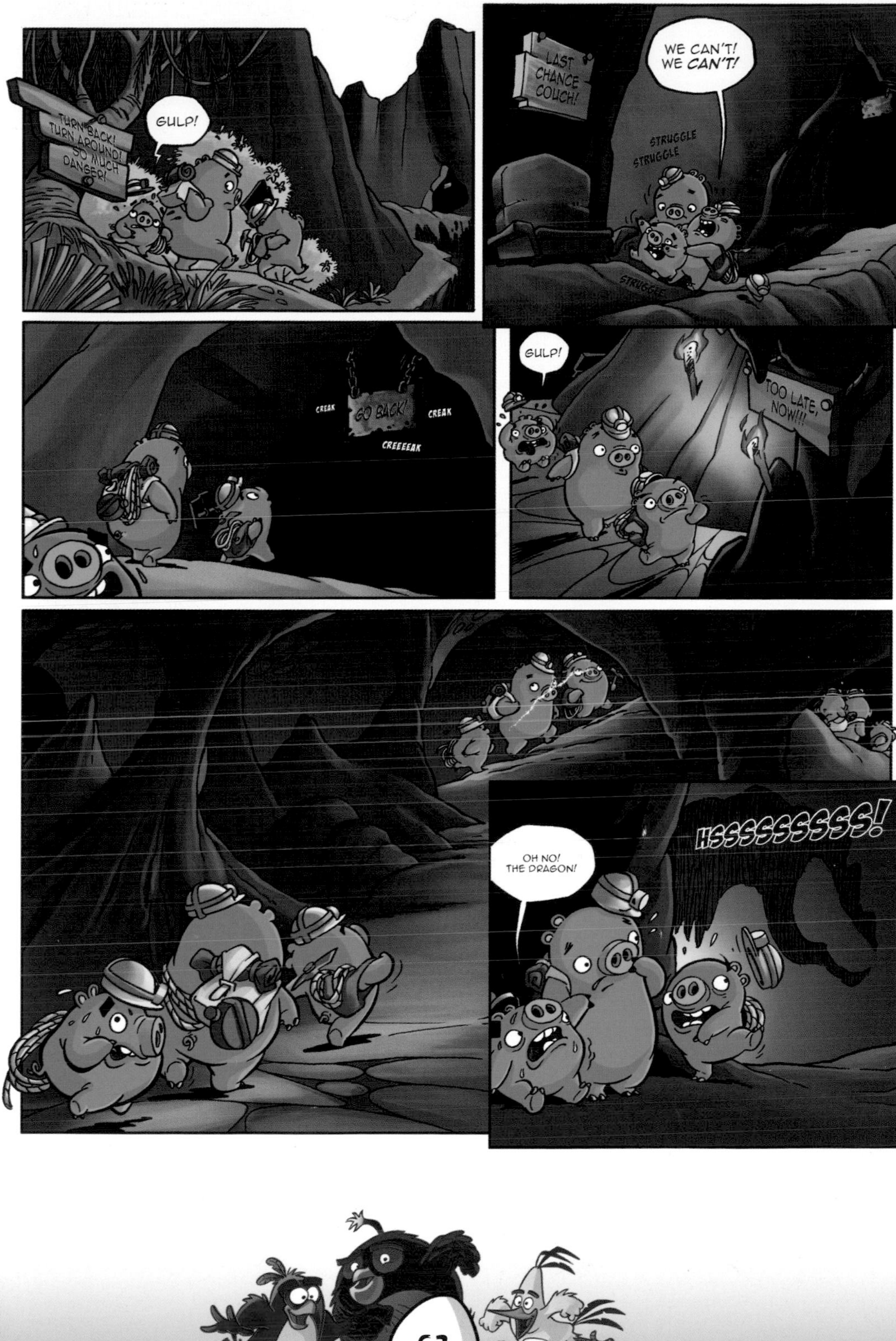
TURN BACK!
TURN AROUND!
SO MUCH
DANGER!
GULP!
LAST
CHANCE
COUCH!
WE CAN'T!
WE CAN'T!
STRUGGLE
STRUGGLE
CREAK
GO BACK!
CREAK
CREEEEAK
GULP!
TOO LATE,
NOW!!!
OH NO!
THE DRAGON!
HSSSSSSSSS!

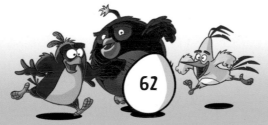

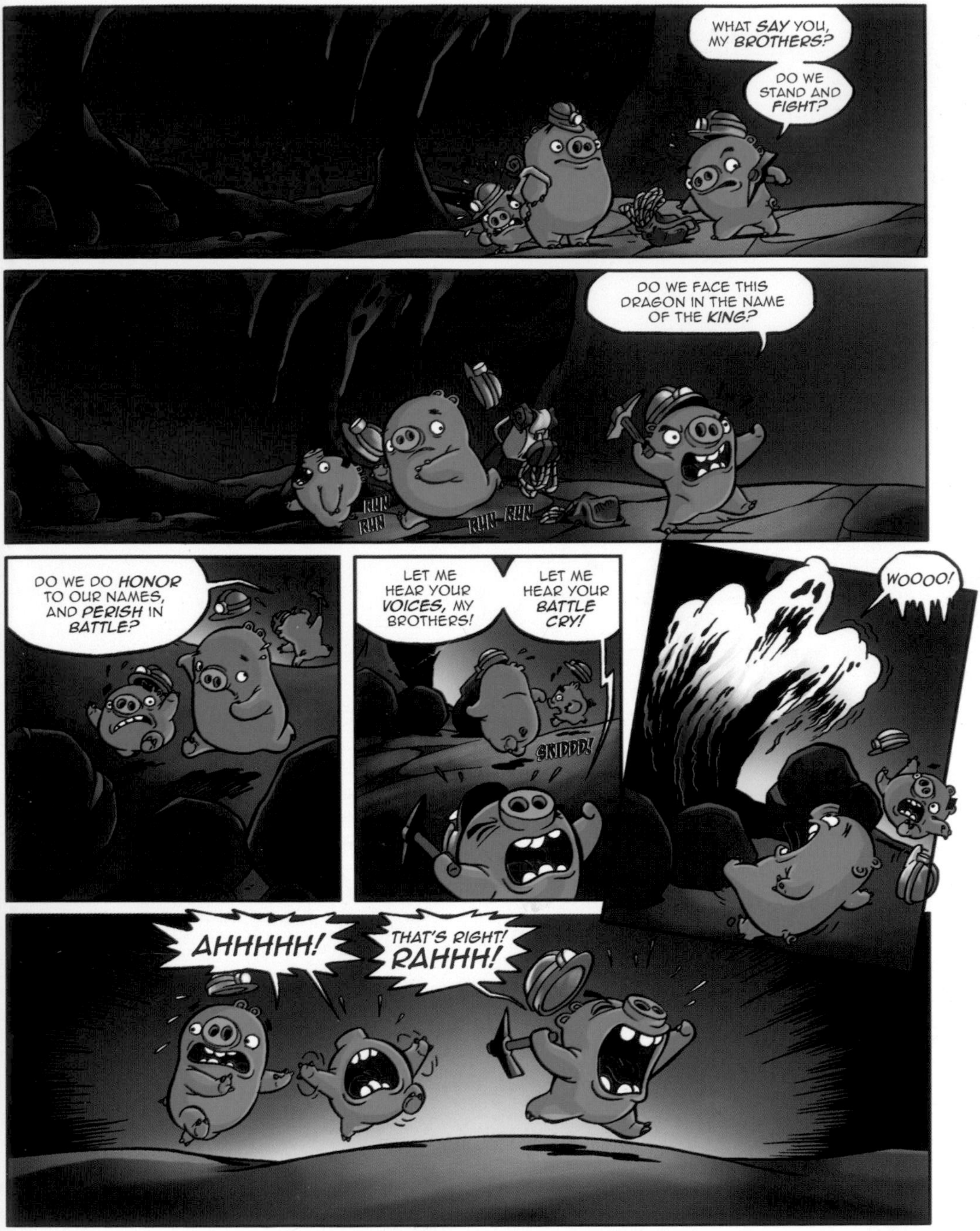
WHAT SAY YOU, MY BROTHERS?
DO WE STAND AND FIGHT?
DO WE FACE THIS DRAGON IN THE NAME OF THE KING?
RUN RUN
RUN RUN
DO WE DO HONOR TO OUR NAMES, AND PERISH IN BATTLE?
LET ME HEAR YOUR VOICES, MY BROTHERS!
LET ME HEAR YOUR BATTLE CRY!
SKIDDD!
WOOOO!
AHHHHH!
THAT'S RIGHT! RAHHH!

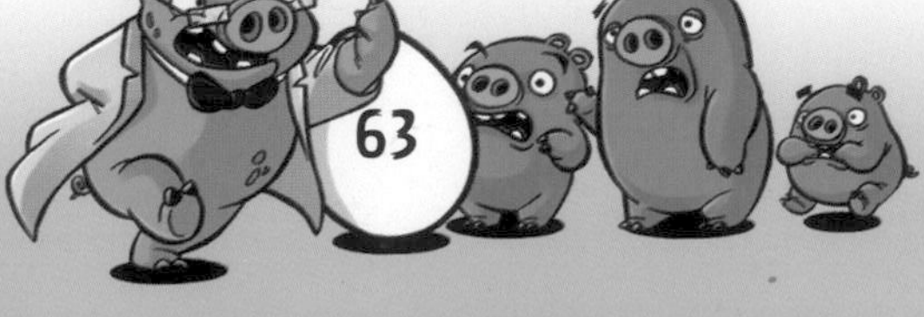

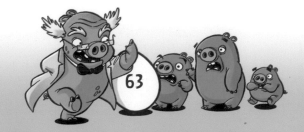

?
OOF.
AHHH!
AND SO...
HSSSSSSSSS!
WOOO
OOOO
OOO!
HSSSSSSSSS!
RUN
RUN
RUN
TROT
TROT
TROT
TROT
TREMBLE
TREMBLE
TREMBLE
TREMBLE

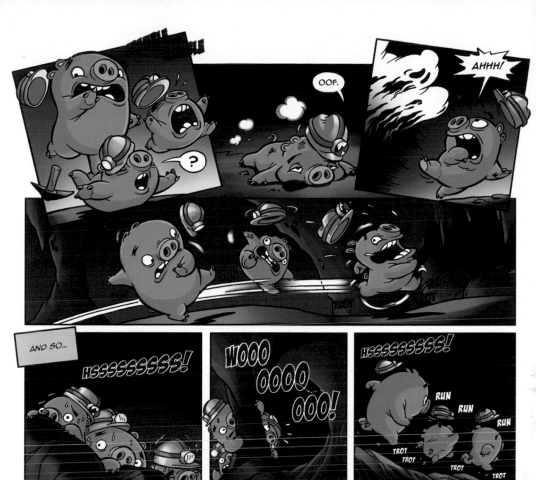

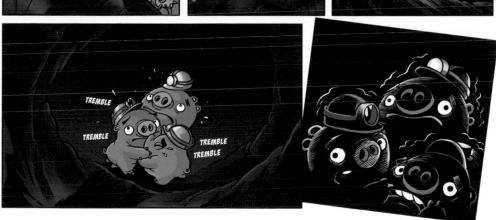

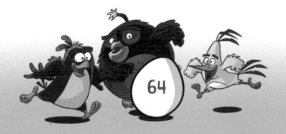

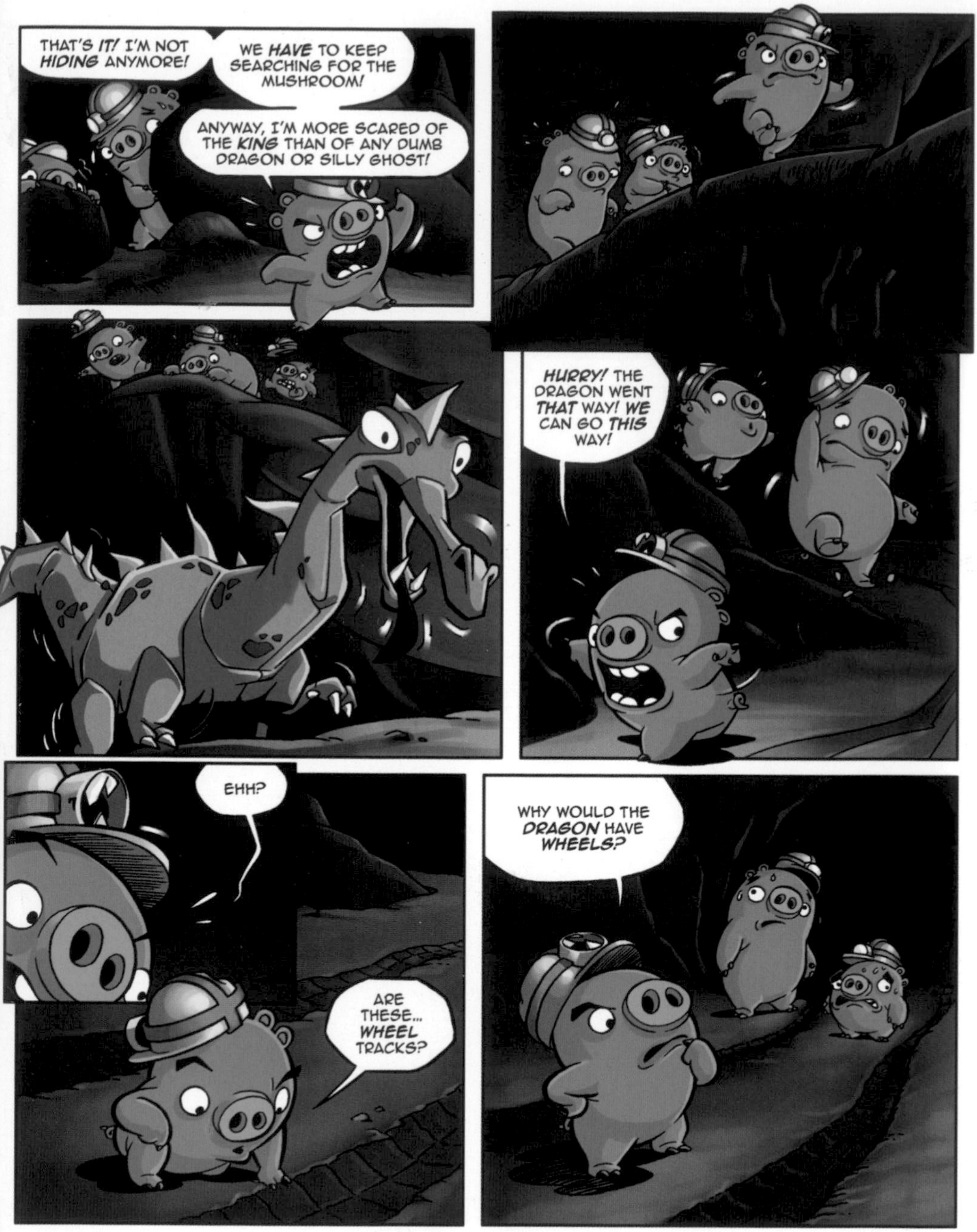

THAT'S IT! I'M NOT HIDING ANYMORE!
WE HAVE TO KEEP SEARCHING FOR THE MUSHROOM!
ANYWAY, I'M MORE SCARED OF THE KING THAN OF ANY DUMB DRAGON OR SILLY GHOST!
HURRY! THE DRAGON WENT THAT WAY! WE CAN GO THIS WAY!
EHH?
ARE THESE... WHEEL TRACKS?
WHY WOULD THE DRAGON HAVE WHEELS?

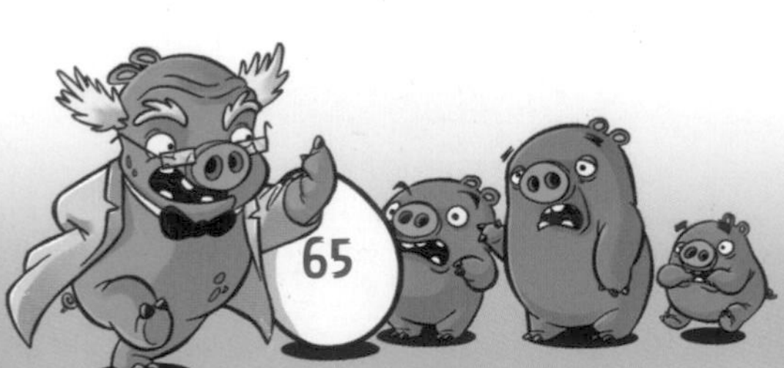

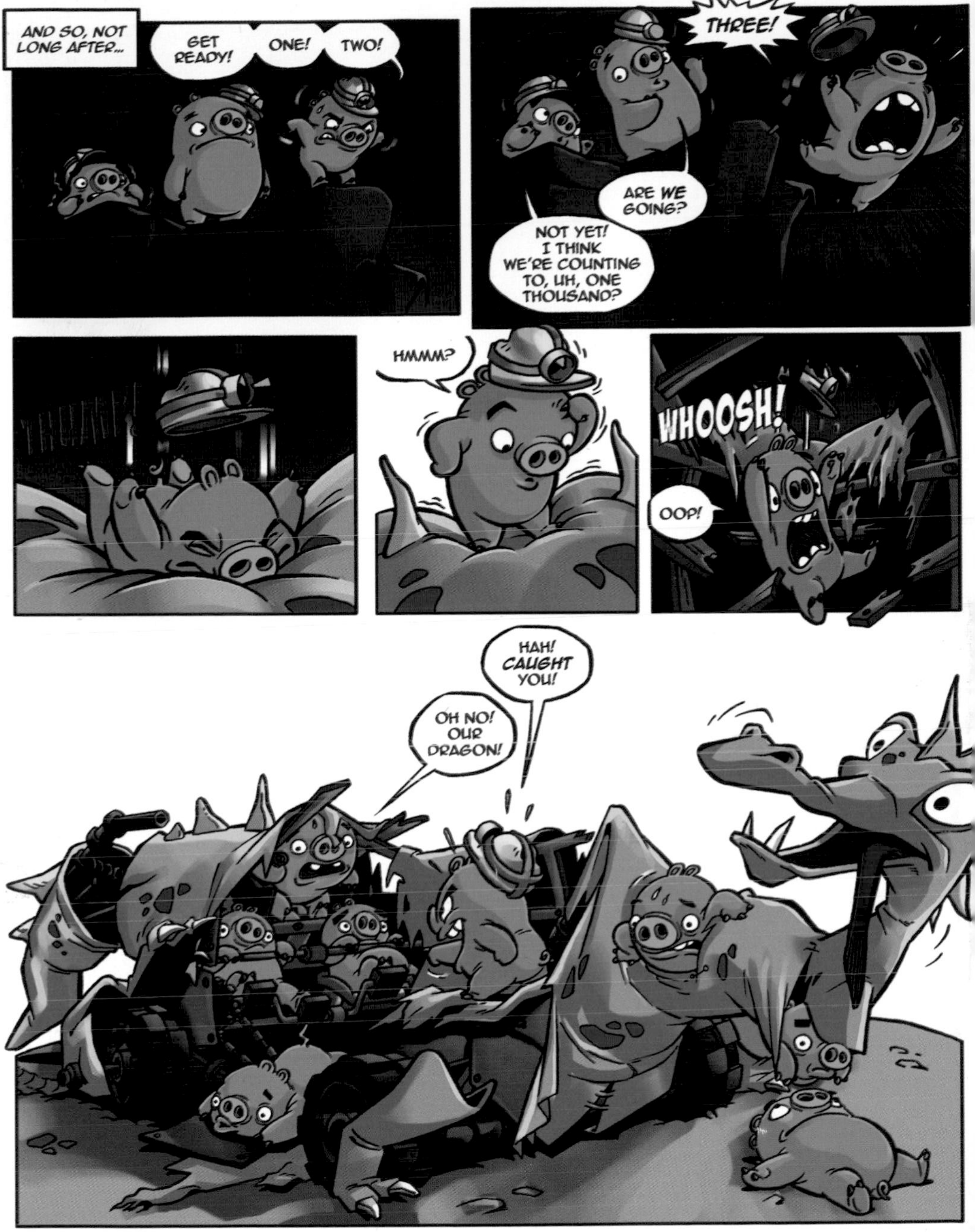
AND SO, NOT LONG AFTER...
GET READY!
ONE!
TWO!
THREE!
ARE WE GOING?
NOT YET! I THINK WE'RE COUNTING TO, UH, ONE THOUSAND?
HMMM?
WHOOSH!
OOP!
OH NO! OUR DRAGON!
HAH! CAUGHT YOU!

AND *YOU'RE* NOT A GHOST! YOU'RE...

...JUST AN OLD BEDSHEET!

HAH! I CAUGHT YOU *ALL!*

WHAT DID YOU *DO* ALL THIS FOR? WHY WERE YOU TRYING TO *SCARE* US?

UH... WE JUST THOUGHT IF WE SCARED *YOU* AWAY, THEN WE COULD FIND THE MUSHROOM, AND THE KING WOULD GIVE *US* THE REWARD.

MEANWHILE...

ONE THOU-SAND!

??

WHOOSH!

??

?

FOUND A PORKINI MUSHROOM!

67

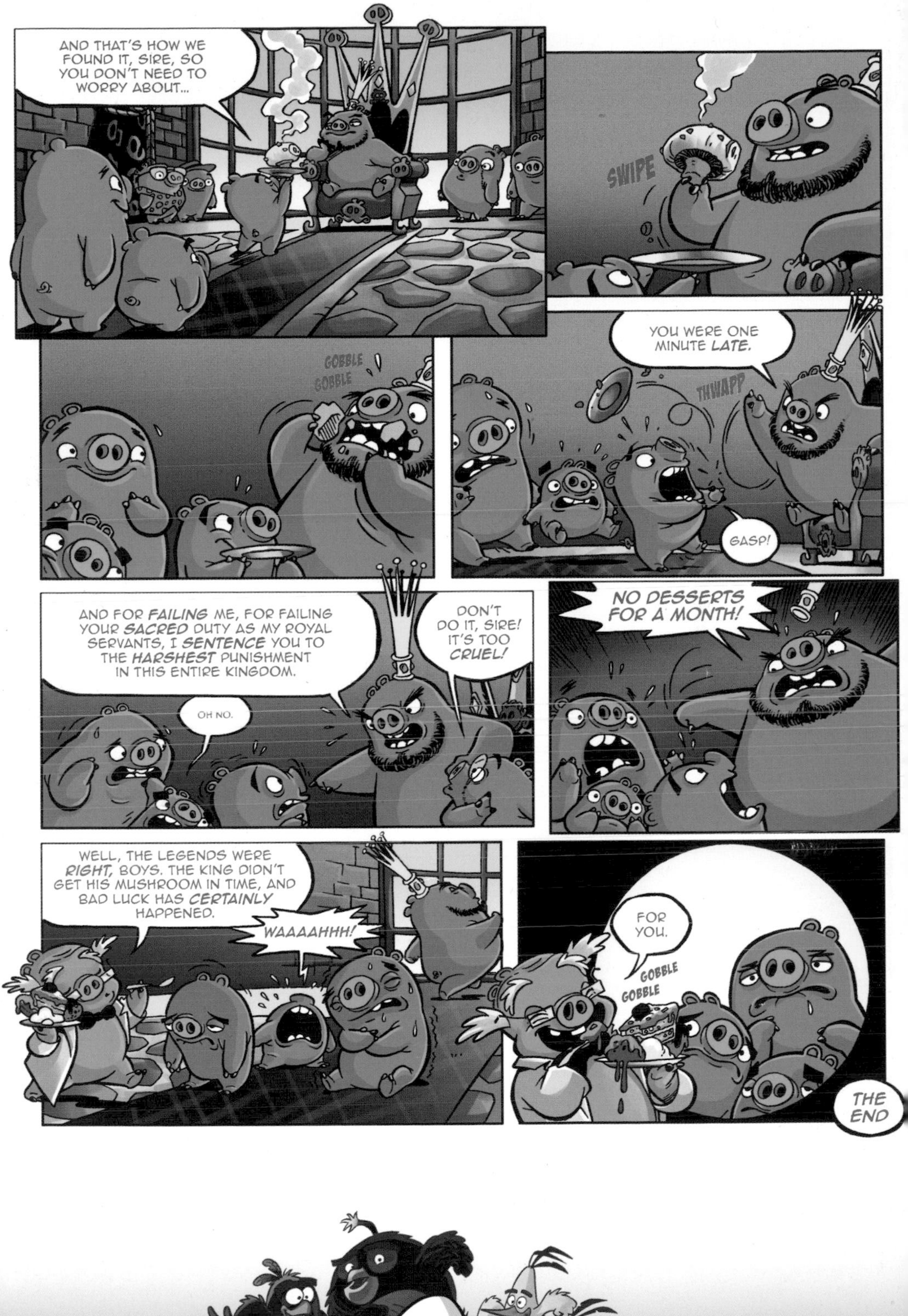
AND THAT'S HOW WE FOUND IT, SIRE, SO YOU DON'T NEED TO WORRY ABOUT...
SWIPE
GOBBLE GOBBLE
YOU WERE ONE MINUTE LATE.
THWAPP
GASP!
AND FOR FAILING ME, FOR FAILING YOUR SACRED DUTY AS MY ROYAL SERVANTS, I SENTENCE YOU TO THE HARSHEST PUNISHMENT IN THIS ENTIRE KINGDOM.
DON'T DO IT, SIRE! IT'S TOO CRUEL!
OH NO.
NO DESSERTS FOR A MONTH!
WELL, THE LEGENDS WERE RIGHT, BOYS. THE KING DIDN'T GET HIS MUSHROOM IN TIME, AND BAD LUCK HAS CERTAINLY HAPPENED.
WAAAAHHH!
FOR YOU.
GOBBLE GOBBLE
THE END

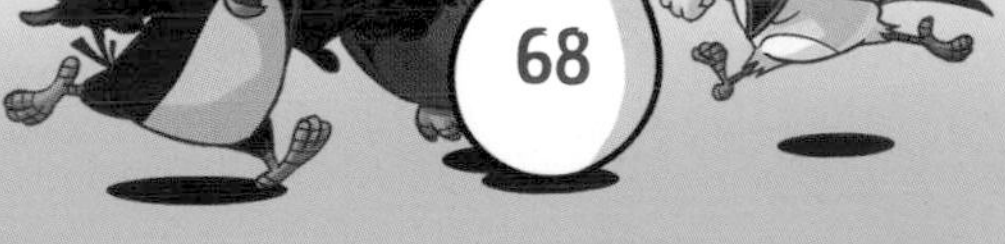

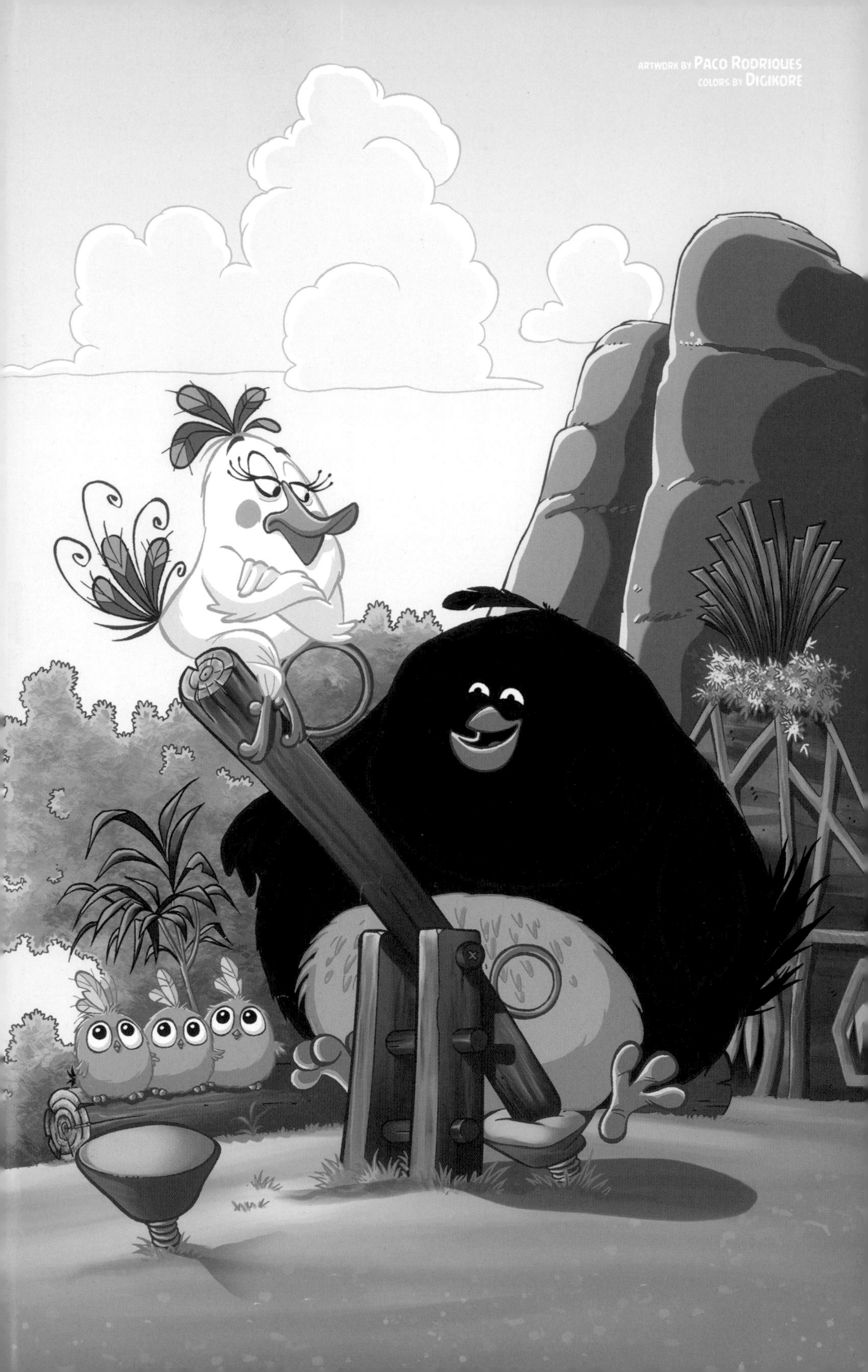
ARTWORK BY PACO RODRIQUES
COLORS BY DIGIKORE

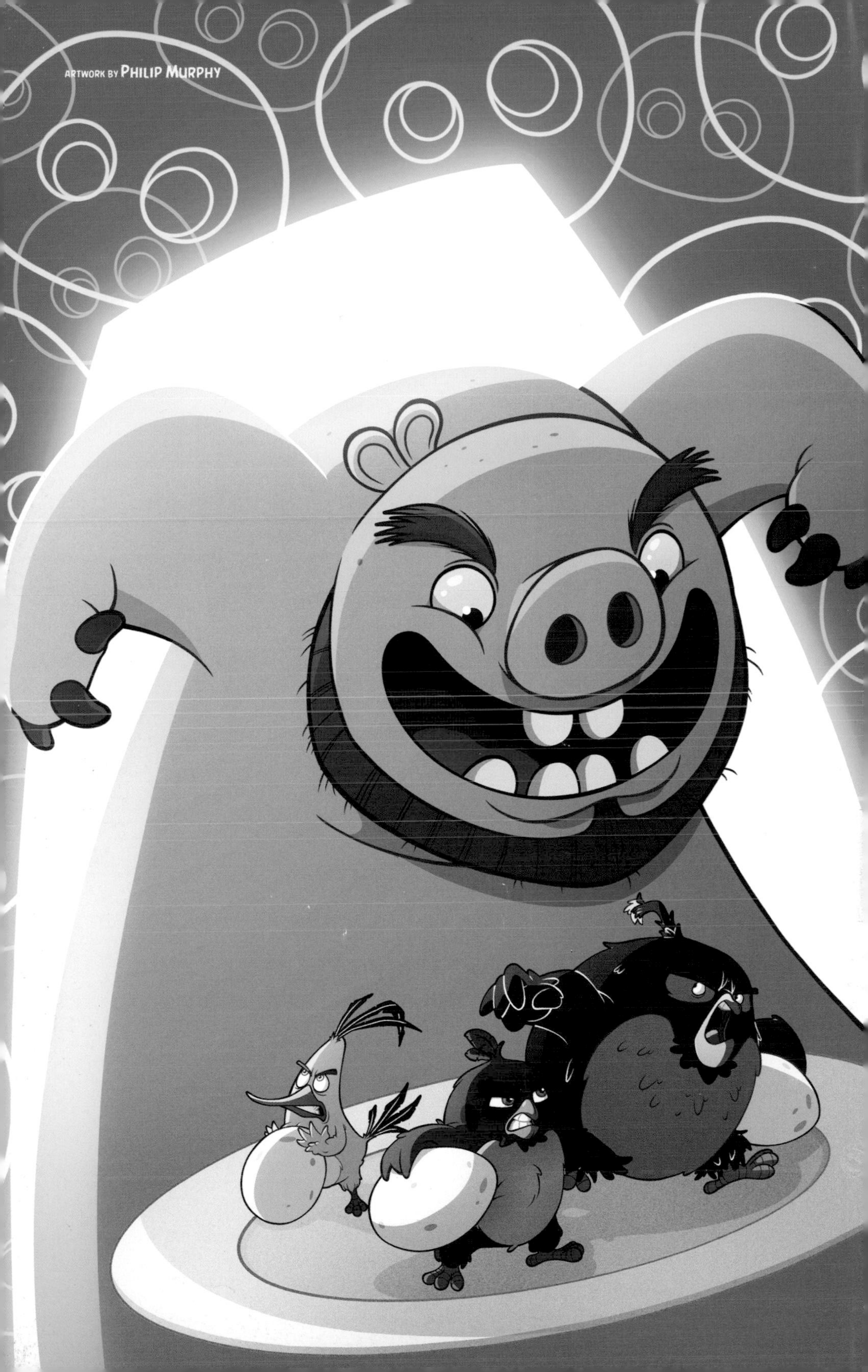
ARTWORK BY PHILIP MURPHY

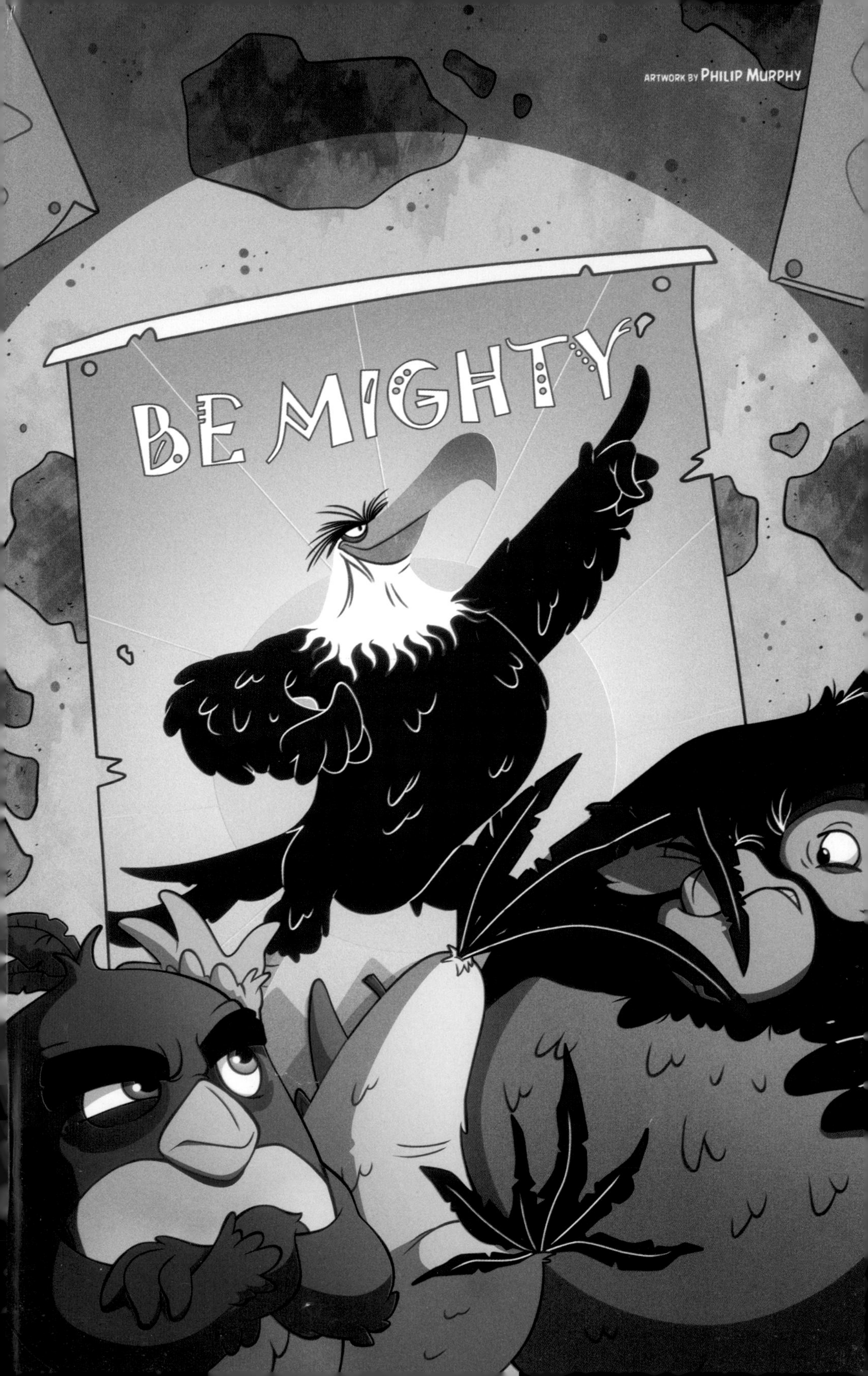
ARTWORK BY PHILIP MURPHY
BE MIGHTY

ARTWORK BY **PACO RODRIQUES**
COLORS BY **DIGIKORE**

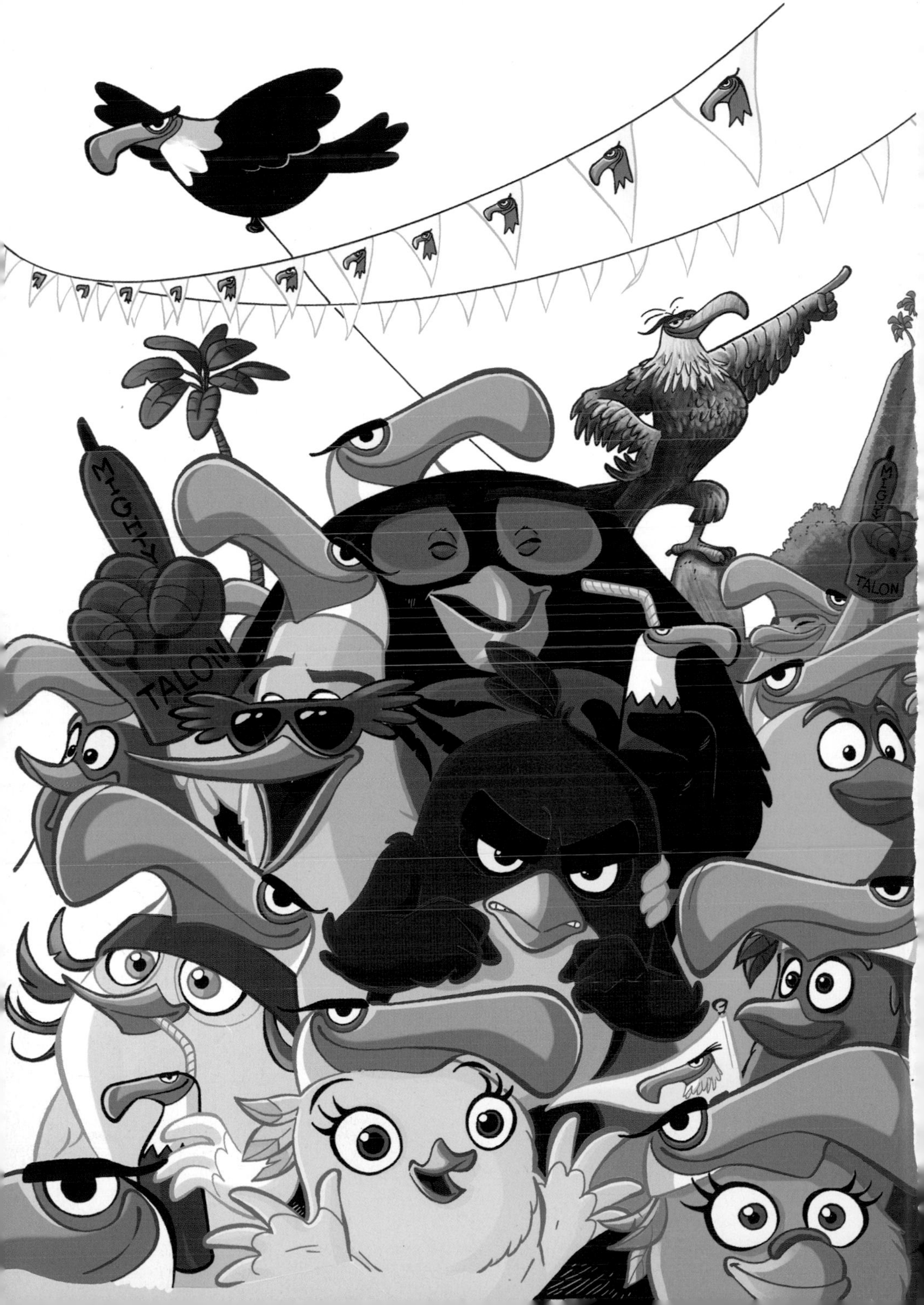
MIGHTY
TALON
MIGHTY
TALON